DEADLY APPETITES

RALEIGH DAVIS

CHAPTER 1

"You were lying back there."

At Cassian's words, my head whips around, my wide-eyed attention coming full force on him. As usual, he's infuriatingly handsome. Mostly because he knows it.

It's in his smile, faint and knowing, as it clings to his sensual mouth. I feel itchy, shivering under my skin when I see that smile. And since we're sharing a very small car, I can't not see it.

I shouldn't have agreed to help him. I shouldn't have agreed to a ride with him. I shouldn't have thought any of this would ever work.

"I don't know what you mean." My back stiffens in the old remembered lines, my body pretending that I'm still an officer in the US Army. Since I'm in civvies, I probably just look uptight. "I said I would help."

I do know what he means though—he doesn't need my help. I never really expected him to accept it, only we were in front of his friends and mine, and the idea I've had rattling around my brain since I met him suddenly grabbed my tongue. He couldn't refuse me in the moment.

I'm not sure if he's refusing me now or only mocking me.

"That's not what I meant." He sounds like he's privately

laughing at me. "You don't give a shit what's inside that thing. So why are you so eager to get inside it?"

I glance into the back seat where the source of this whole insane situation I've put myself in is sitting. A black metal box is on the seat, dusty and scratched. It's filled with electrical components and loaded with a program that Cassian designed with five of his friends years ago. The box is meant to turn an ordinary car into a self-driving one.

The box probably also killed Cassian's mentor. It's been lost ever since Ira drove off Highway 1 and died along with Cassian's friend Tynan. Except it turns out Tynan might be alive and might be responsible for the box mysteriously appearing in Cassian's office a few days ago.

I shouldn't be in this car with him. Cassian and his friends are billionaires, and I'm only a former Army Signal Corps officer. Yes, my best friend has fallen in love with one of Cassian's friends, and she's even more deeply involved in this mystery than ever before... but when Cassian announced he was going to find whatever secrets were in the box, I should've kept my mouth shut.

Instead, I volunteered to help him. And then I accepted a ride home from him.

Cassian is exactly the kind of man I'm allergic to: arrogantly knowing, smugly mocking, as if the entire world is a joke to him. But sharply charming too. He's a marketing genius, and he knows how to get people to do what he wants.

He's also exactly the kind of man I keep falling for—with disastrous results—and I don't understand why. Which is why I volunteered my help, even though he's right—I don't really care what's inside, and I don't have any specialized knowledge that might help him.

I straighten my back, remind myself of the true reason I'm here. "Okay, you're right. I don't give a damn about that box or whatever you guys did to it. But I do care about Tess." I leave that as a reasonable explanation for why I'm here and skip ahead to details, hoping he'll leave it there. "We can meet whenever you want. I have to work during the day, and my Saturday mornings aren't free, but otherwise I'm available."

It takes me a moment to realize how that sounds. As if I've got nothing else going on in my life. Definitely no romantic partner to occupy me.

He's probably already got a date scheduled for tonight. And a hookup for tomorrow. And an assignation all weekend.

"I also have a job," he points out.

He's got more than a job. He's a billionaire CEO of the world's most powerful marketing firm. He's revolutionized advertising.

"I'm sure you can set your own hours."

"You'd be surprised," he murmurs. "What do you do on Saturday mornings?"

I take abandoned dogs to go play with foster kids. I can already see him sneering at that, his full upper lip curling to reveal a flash of strong white teeth. Cassian isn't wholesome or charitable. He'd probably think I'm some kind of bleeding-heart do-gooder. Maybe he already does.

But the kids need the comfort and so do the dogs, and someone's got to do it. If not me, who? No one else had even thought of such a program before I suggested it. Most Saturdays it's just me bringing the dogs, helping with the kids. I'm not complaining, but if I stop, the program will too.

"I have a commitment," I say through a tight jaw.

He raises an eyebrow. "Really? But you said whenever I wanted."

The way his voice curves around *I wanted* sends a shiver through me. He must have practiced saying it just that way— it can't be natural. He's too damn good at it.

I shake off my reaction. "Well, within those limits."

"Mmm." He flashes me a look from those intense eyes. "You like limits. You're very precise. Stern."

He makes that sound unbearably sexy. Like he was describing my body and not my inflexible personality.

I force air in and out through my nose. I'm not some shrinking Victorian virgin. I was an officer in the US Army, deployed to Afghanistan, for heaven's sake.

"Yes." I do that in my best commanding officer voice, hoping it works on him. "So my limits are any times or days but those."

"I can work with that." Again, I sense that he's laughing at me. Was he mocking me in that sexy tone when he was talking about my being precise and stern and correct?

The thought makes my heart want to split. My pride is definitely bruised. But I'd better get used to it if I'm going to move forward with this plan.

I'm not great with men who are wickedly handsome and know exactly what effect they have on people. In fact, I'm downright terrible. They make me nervous, on edge, unable to think clearly. Flustered.

I *hate* being flustered. And Cassian flusters me with the power and ferocity of a fricking hurricane.

But I'm going to learn how he does it and armor myself against him and all the other men like him. Men like my ex, who shattered my confidence with a few simple words.

Never again. I won't be hurt like that. *Know your enemy*—that's a pretty key rule of engagement. I'm going to *engage* Cassian, learn his tactics, and neutralize his effect on me.

Once I'm done, I'll have nothing to fear from bad boys ever again.

But I can't talk about that or the box or my real reasons for being in this car with him. How to explain that I'm really only here to learn how to avoid him like the plague? I take a deep breath, searching for something to talk about. What would I have in common with a billionaire? Nothing. And he doesn't strike me as a dog lover.

"So, do you have any cats?"

He gives me a look like he wasn't expecting that. At all. "I do," he says slowly. "Two. Did Tess tell you about them?"

It's my turn to be surprised. "Really? *You* have cats?"

"Why are you so shocked?" His eyes narrow. "It's not strange to own cats. Do you have one?"

I shift because he's right—I am overreacting. Except he doesn't seem like he'd care about anything but himself and making money—he definitely wouldn't care about a cat. "I was only making conversation," I say stiffly, mad at myself for screwing this up.

Cassian stares out the windshield, his hands tight on the steering wheel. He doesn't say anything for so long my heart starts to pound.

"What are your cats' names?" I ask finally.

"Bruiser and Bane."

"Wow. Are they fighting cats?"

He busts out laughing. "No. They're strays I took in. Bruiser is massive, like twenty pounds, and loves to sit right on your chest, the better to suffocate you. Bane is a skinny shadow who's missing an ear and a toe and avoids everyone."

The affection in his voice makes my skin tingle warmly. He really loves his large sons.

"Why don't you put them on your Instagram?" I ask. "People would love them."

"That's not the brand," he says shortly.

Right, because he's a *brand*. He has to be Cassian, model-hot tech titan, in order to sell things to people. And to seduce people into his bed. No one can know he's got two cats he loves—then he couldn't manipulate people with his curated image.

"God forbid you drop the Instagram thot brand," I mutter.

He chokes. "Excuse me?"

"A thirst trap." I wave my hand at all his too-cool masculine energy. "Or whatever they call it now. You post pictures, knowing they'll get attention."

"Are you stalking my Instagram?" Wicked delight curls through his tone.

"It's a public account," I say stiffly. "And I keep seeing it on the Explore page. The algorithm must be broken."

"Right," he drawls. "The algorithm… that's curated based on accounts you look at. *Frequently.*"

"I do *not* follow you."

"But you see me anyway." His smile widens. "So, what's your Instagram handle?"

"It's private." It's actually not, but I don't want him to find me. I haven't posted much. The thought of putting pictures of myself out for the entire world to see is… Ugh. Just ugh. Mostly I post pictures of the dogs because they need the attention. Several have found forever homes that way.

"Mmm." He sounds intrigued.

"I promise you wouldn't like it," I say with as much ice as I can generate. The thought of this man, with his too-easy charm, seeing my doggie IG makes me want to squirm, as if he'd be seeing my soft underbelly instead.

"You'd be surprised at what I like." He's not put off at all, darn it. "What, is it all food pics? Outfits? Hair tutorials?"

I snort because my hair is always, always pulled up in a ponytail. I have the most boring hair on earth. "Yeah, I do a ponytail of the day in my grid. People eat it up."

"I'm sure they do." He's looking at my ponytail in a way that makes me think about him running his hand through it, the brown strands slipping across his spread fingers like silk. He catches me watching him and his expression shifts. "Look, if you dislike me so much," he says finally, "why did you agree to help? And don't say anything about an obsolete connector or helping Tess. So why?"

I search for a lie, even though he's proved he can tell when I am. But I'm no good at lying—in fact, I almost can't do it. Like, physically, telling something untrue is like trying to pull my own teeth.

"The last guy I dated was like you," I blurt out, choosing the truth almost instinctively. If I can't lie, I might as well use the truth. He already thinks my interest and my reserve and my dislike is a joke. Fine. I'll give him the whole punch line.

It's going to be terribly, horribly embarrassing to admit this, but better to be humiliated now and protected later. Besides, Cassian is the king of the bad boys. There will be no better example for me to learn from. I can't let this opportunity get away.

He's so surprised the car actually swerves before he quickly brings it back under control. "Like *me?*" He snorts, as if it's impossible for any other man in the world to be the superspecial flower he is.

"Yes." I get that out through gritted teeth. "Too charming, slick, and shallow. And the guy I dated before that was the same. And the guy before him." And on and on.

"So you have a type." His smile is so smug it makes my jaw hurt.

"*No.*" I take a deep breath to steady myself, feeling sick to my stomach. This is going worse than I imagined. "That's the point. They all ended in disaster. Utter disaster."

The first simply ghosted me. The second told me in a very casual way that I was just, you know, *kind of boring.*

The last took great pleasure in telling me I was way too uptight to fuck. My face heats just remembering. God, it might have been the most humiliating moment of my life.

No, it was. I went home and was sick immediately after. My body betrayed me as I knelt on the cold tile floor, helpless against the anguished shame of it all.

I never want that to happen again. Which is where Cassian comes in.

"That makes total sense," he says tightly. "You hate guys like *me,* so you volunteered to help and therefore be in close proximity to me. Perfectly logical."

"I want to know how you do it," I say. "I want to see how you operate from the inside out."

I've thought a lot about this since the moment I first met Cassian at Gideon's place several weeks ago. I saw immediately what kind of man he was. And I was also immediately, uncomfortably attracted to him. So I resolved then and there to fix this. Fix myself.

"Operate." He says it slowly, like I've just accused him of a crime. But he has to know how he is. After all, it's part of *his brand*.

"Yes." I nod firmly. "I want to know exactly how you do it, your whole..." I gesture dismissively at him. "Your whole *thing*."

"My thing," he repeats, his voice dangerously soft. "That thing I do that you hate but can't resist."

"Exactly." I nod sharply. "I want to be able to identify men like you and my exes at a thousand yards. So I never date one of you ever again."

CHAPTER 2

I have never in my life had a woman say that to me. My mouth falls open, which is something I never let myself do. It looks idiotic, but I can't help it.

"You want me to show you how to avoid guys like me?" My voice is too strained, and I quickly wrestle it back under control.

Okay, maybe a few women have said something like that to me. But as a joke mostly. Like, *I can tell you'll be bad for me* said with a sly smile and maybe a finger trailed across my tie. And then they found out just how good I am at being bad for them.

They always say goodbye with a smile though, and I'm fucking offended Victoria makes it sound like I've got the plague.

"No." She speaks in that careful, upright tone of hers, as precise as her posture. "I want to observe you as you try to date me so that I can catalog how you do it. And therefore I can identify your tactics in the future and avoid them."

Tin Soldier. It's what I started calling her privately when I first met her. She looks like she should be in a crisp set of pink and greens, reviewing a line of troops, ready to rally them into battle. Iron jaw, ramrod spine, narrowed gaze—she's like an Army stock photo come to life.

But there're hints of softness in her too. She can't compress those full lips of hers no matter how hard she tries. And a few wisps of honey-blond hair always escape her ponytail, framing her high cheekbones.

The contrasts are like a drug to me. I can't stop wanting to look at her. To plumb just how far those contrasts go. Is she soft when she kisses? Or steely? What about when she's on the edge of an orgasm?

But I knew she doesn't like me, so I didn't press it. I might be a bad boy, but I'm not that bad. Despite what Miss Tin Soldier thinks of me.

And now she wants me to try to date her. As if I were a crash-test dummy, ready to flail and break at her command.

"Why would I do that?" I put some ice on the edge of my words. "My time is valuable."

Her cheeks go pale, but she doesn't flinch. "Because I'm helping you with the car computer."

"I don't need your help. I designed it myself—I can take it apart myself."

"That was years ago. And you didn't do it on your own. When's the last time you touched a piece of hardware even?"

I snort. "I've forgotten more about that machine than you could ever learn about it."

She flinches. Good. Her hands curl into fists. "I want to protect myself, okay? And I *can* help you with it. I'm not sucking up your valuable time without offering something in return."

There's a mix of defiant defensiveness and utter vulnerability in her that just cracks me wide open. Not that I'll show her, because she's right—that's not the brand. I suppose we can do some kind of tit-for-tat thing. A second set of hands on the car computer would be helpful, and I bet she learns fast.

Although I don't do fake anything. And I'm already way too intrigued by her to make this as safe and bloodless as she wants it to be.

"What if you fall for me?" I slide her a look. "You already know you have a weakness for men like me. What if in all this fake dating, your feelings become real?"

Her cheeks go so red I almost feel like an ass. "That won't happen."

"Are you sure?" I make my voice smoother than silk, the better to fluster her. If she can't handle me like this, she'll never last the full treatment. "Those other guys are nothing compared to me. They're cherry bombs. I'm the MOAB."

Her breathing has gone odd and she's staring out the window, her lips parted. "Comparing yourself to ordnance is so ridiculous."

"Just wanted to put it into terms you'd understand."

She turns her head for long moments, leaving me with only a view of the line of her neck, the curl of her ear, the slope of her shoulder. She's composing herself and I wanted her upset, so I shouldn't feel this fucking awful about it.

Slowly she folds her hands together in her lap. Her spine gets even straighter, a thing I didn't know was possible, and she turns back to me. Her mouth is flat, her cheeks pale, but her eyes burn.

"This is important to me." The gravity in her voice is a force I can't resist. "I want to meet someone I can make a life with. But men like you keep ruining it."

Jesus. I have to take a breath, then another, because I've never been described like the plague before. Or a deadly allergy.

I have a cousin who's allergic to onions. Imagine everything you cook that has onions in it, how many recipes start with "Brown some diced onions." He can't eat any of it. But of course accidents happen and sometimes he has to deploy his EpiPen.

He once told me "Things taste better with onions" with such sadness in his tone. I've never forgotten it.

"So I'm going to be your onions," I mutter to myself.

"Pardon?"

So fucking typical. No matter how much money I earn, how much I make myself over, I'm still just grifting trash in the end. Not worthy of being around decent people, only out to scam people out of their hard-earned cash… or sell them something they don't need or can't attain.

Little Miss Tin Soldier hates me, but she also can't resist me. And she isn't above using me for her own ends.

Maybe I deserve it though. I did get my start scamming people out of money—and I was damn good at it. Always have been. At least now I do it legitimately.

The man who saw me and thought I could do more and be more with my talents… Well, I helped design that box behind us, which probably killed him along with one of my best friends. Ira was… I mean, I have a dad, and he's fine. We're not exactly close, not since he pretty much gave up on me when I was a teenager. The money I brought in with my scams helped keep the lights and my siblings fed, but my dad made sure to let me know how dirty he thought that money was. And he was right—it was dirty.

He's more than happy to take my money now that it's "clean." I'm still using the same tactics I was before, but somehow being this fucking rich makes everything I do right and moral suddenly.

Except to Victoria. She's turned away from me like she might catch my filthiness.

She wants a charming shitbag to wine and dine her? To pull every trick in the book to seduce her? Well, she's going to get a lot more than she bargained for. Because I'll pull out all the stops for her.

"I said," I announce in a loud, ringing tone, "I'll help you.

You want a bad boy you can't resist?" I smile, showing just enough teeth to put an edge of worry in her expression. "Well, you've got him. Hope you're ready."

CHAPTER 3

I'm not ready.

There's no way I can say that out loud, because this entire thing was my idiot idea. The way he's smiling at me… I'm hot and cold all at once, my heart racing, then stalling, before going off again.

He's literally giving me heart palpitations just from a smile. This is going to be bad.

No. I shake my head. This is going to be good because I'm going to seize this chance. I lean over, studying him closely. "How do you do that? That smile. Because it's definitely practiced."

The smile drops like a stone. "I don't make faces at myself in the mirror."

"But it's not real. How do you do it if it's not real?"

"Don't you ever smile when you don't mean it?"

All the time. When I'm with people I don't know well, it feels like that's the only kind of smile I can produce.

I've never faked a smile with Cassian though. Rather than dwell too deeply on that unsettling thought, I go on. "But you're *good* at it."

"If I'm so good, why did you think it was fake? It wasn't, but we'll get into that later."

I blink and think about it. How did I figure out that there was something off about his smile? "You… you wanted me to feel a very specific way. Unsettled. Maybe you even wanted me to rethink the whole thing."

"But you did feel that way. So certainly the reaction it provoked was real."

I cross my arms. "This is my point. It's all manipulation, and I hate it."

He snorts. "Of course it's all manipulation. That doesn't make it fake. When you were talking with Tess about Gideon —and I know you were—you wanted to make her feel a certain way. You probably wanted to warn her away from him, didn't you?"

Of course I wanted to and of course I did. Tess is supremely happy with Gideon, and I get the feeling he would probably die for her, but… Well, the situation at first wasn't good, not with keeping her practically captive and the break-ins and the recluse act. "Anyone in their right mind would have warned her off. I mean, she told me even you came by and read him the riot act."

He sighs as he pulls the car into a shaded driveway. I suddenly notice that we've arrived at a gorgeous mansion in Saint Francis Wood on a lot big enough and with enough trees that it's almost private. Which is quite a feat in cramped San Francisco. There's a wrought iron fence around the entire estate, enclosing the forest that surrounds the house. It very much says *No, you may* not *come in.*

"Is this your house?" I ask. "I thought you were taking me home."

He stops the car at the front entrance. "We're getting started now."

Heat washes through me as I imagine exactly what we might start. His hands on me, his lips trailing over my skin—

I sit bolt upright. *Holy shit.* He's going to try to seduce me physically too. It won't just be dates and flirting; he's going to touch me. Intimately.

This is something I should have planned for. I mean, I knew somewhere in the back of my mind this would have to happen, but imagining it… I can't catch my breath, and I'm so overheated I can melt an iceberg.

"Are we starting on the computer?" My voice is pitched higher than normal. I struggle to drag it back down. "Or…?"

Although this was all my idea, I can't finish that. Instead, I press my mouth shut tight and let myself go blank-faced.

Cassian still gives me a knowing look. He can work those brown eyes like no other. "Or are we getting to work on you?" The way he curls his voice around me makes my toes curl. "I was thinking both. Unless you have somewhere to be?"

I should say yes since he so clearly thinks I don't. But I can't lie—anytime I try to, I end up choking on my own tongue. And if I did that, he'd give me another of those knowing looks.

"No time like the present." I reach for the door handle.

"Wait." His tone is mild, but it's definitely a command. "First lesson: I open the door for you. Always."

Even as my pulse accelerates, I bristle. "I can open my own door."

"That's not the point." His voice remains smooth as silk. "The point is I want to touch you. To feel your entire weight balanced in my hand."

I lick my lips, unable to look away from him. "I… I thought you'd just want to look at my legs as I got out."

A brief flash of a smile. "And that too. Don't move."

He comes around the car with quick grace and is opening the door for me before I can reconsider waiting for him. His hand stretches toward me, his fingers long and elegant. I take a deep breath and put my palm into his.

I'm glad I got some oxygen in me before I did, because my

brain starts to short-circuit, neurons snapping and popping like firecrackers. His skin is surprisingly warm, his grip firm and reassuring.

One more inhale just to clear my head, and then I swing my legs out. His gaze runs over them, brief but appreciative. And then he's lifting me up.

As I'm balanced between him and the seat, I realize that with one sharp tug he can pull me right into him. I'm certain he'd catch me easily, and then we'd be pressed tight together, touching from chest to hip. When he inhaled, I'd *feel* it. If he pulled me into him.

He doesn't. Instead, he sets me on my feet and releases my hand. "I'll meet you inside. It's unlocked."

As he reaches into the back seat for the computer, I fully take in the house. It's sleek and modern with lots of glass and exposed metal but with touches of classical elements too, like the columns holding up the portico and the details above the windows. The colors are muted, but on the lighter side—I was expecting something darker. Something that screamed sex den.

This house doesn't need to brag about its elegance. It's as coolly confident as its owner.

The front door opens as I approach. A middle-aged man in business casual is on the other side.

"Miss Shepherd, welcome." He's got the faintest hint of a posh accent. "Mr. Aubert told me you'd be visiting us." He nods to Cassian, who's coming up behind me. "Everything's set in the living room."

"Thank you, Lawford," Cassian says. "Victoria, this is my..." He cocks his head. "Would you call yourself a butler?"

Lawford smiles faintly. "Perhaps a factotum? I don't know that the butlers I've met would claim me as one of their own."

I notice then that he's got a hardness about him, like he doesn't exactly spend his days polishing the silver. Is he Cassian's bodyguard?

"He keeps everything running around here," Cassian tells me. He puts a hand in the small of my back, and I have to bite off a sharp inhale. Even through my shirt, his touch sizzles. "The living room is this way."

The interior of the house echoes the exterior, with high-contrast black-and-white photos on the bright white walls and soft rugs tossed over the marble floors. I slow to get a better look at the pictures, which seem to be sand dunes. Or maybe tree branches?

I narrow my eyes, trying to figure out what exactly the images are. As recognition clicks, a wash of sensations runs along my spine.

Those are people, or rather naked limbs, intertwined. There's a hand on a thigh, an arm draped over a torso, lips pressed against a shoulder. It's not pornographic at all—more like artistically sensual. And there's nothing showing that you wouldn't see in a high-end fashion magazine.

Still, I can't help but feel unsettled when I look at the photos, probably because I've asked this man to show me all his tricks of seduction. These pictures definitely have me imagining things with him. Things very much like the people in the photos are doing.

"Coming?" he asks me blandly, as if he has no idea how those pictures have affected me. And really, it's all thanks to him—I've seen more explicit things in museums and never blushed like a virgin.

I lift my chin, force my expression to harden. "Of course." I don't look at the walls as I follow him.

The living room is smaller than I expected—it's cozy, almost intimate. This isn't a place for massive parties; it's best suited for two people to curl up together. The furniture is luxuriously low-slung. Once you're in one of the chairs, you won't be considering getting up for a while.

In one chair, the most muscular cat I've ever seen is lounging, looking exactly like a miniaturized tiger if a tiger was gray with black stripes. The cat yawns as I approach, revealing teeth to match his size.

"Don't pet him," Cassian says as if doesn't really care if I listen or not. "He's very cruel in his affection."

I decide not to risk it. I'm in enough danger from the cat's owner. "Is this Bruiser?"

"Yes." He gestures for me to take a seat across from Bruiser. I guess the cat isn't safe to sit next to. "We won't see Bane."

The cat blinks his large green eyes at Cassian, and I get the impression that Bruiser tolerates Cassian in this house rather than the other way around.

True to his word, Lawford's set out a pot of tea, finger sandwiches with the crusts cut off, and various sweets. Nothing's meant to be eaten with a fork.

"Thank you, Lawford," Cassian murmurs to him as the man shuts the door behind him.

We're alone.

Before I let myself even process that, I reach for the computer, which Cassian has set on the coffee table. The metal box enclosing it has started to rust at the edges, the switches on it crumbling and orange. But it's in surprisingly good shape for having been fished out of the ocean. I'm reminded of the men who died in the crash, Ira and Tynan.

I glance quickly at Cassian and wonder what kind of awfulness Ira took him away from. Whatever it was, it doesn't show at all in his demeanor—he's the most self-assured man I've ever met.

But then bad things don't dent him. Ira and Tynan crashed off Highway 1 into the Pacific five years ago, killing both of them. Possibly because this computer failed and ran the car off the road. If Cassian feels any guilt about that, he hides it well. Me, I'd be shaking if the evidence I might have killed someone reappeared out of the blue a few days ago.

Tynan, the car, and this computer were supposed to be at

the bottom of the ocean, never to be recovered. They found Ira, but the rest were lost. Until someone started trying to steal the notebooks Ira left them—I still don't quite understand that part—and this computer appeared on Cassian's desk.

Against all odds, it seems that Tynan must have survived. And he's come back to… Well, I'm not sure what he has planned, but it doesn't seem like it's going to be a happy reunion.

So we're going to reconstruct this computer, get it running again, and see if we can figure out exactly what happened.

And Cassian is going to woo me in the meantime. Although he probably never does anything as gentle or weak as *woo*.

I swallow hard. "It wasn't in the water long. I mean, there's rust but not as much as you'd expect."

"You should eat something," he says, taking one of the chairs. Bruiser hops onto his lap for a quick pet, then disappears out of the room. "You didn't touch anything at Gideon's."

"Really, I'm fine." I was too keyed up to do anything at Gideon's besides listen to the remarkable explanation of everything going on. People coming back from the dead doesn't happen every day. I pick up the box, tilt it. "Do you have—?"

"Sit down." He hasn't raised his voice at all, but it rings with command. "Eat something. Tess said you haven't eaten all day."

I look outside and notice that it's gotten dark. Jeez, I really haven't eaten all day. "We should get started though," I say weakly. "The sooner we get this running, the better."

He reaches over and takes the box from me, easily handling it with just one hand. "It took us a year to build this AI and the chips. That doesn't count the testing. We're not going to get to the bottom of it in one evening. And my first rule of seduction: make sure my date is comfortable and satisfied."

I consider arguing more, because I really do want to break this thing open.

"I can't teach you my methods if you don't cooperate." His voice is silky. And deadly.

I wonder what would happen if I keep arguing. Would he call the entire thing off, disassemble and reassemble the computer all on his own? Or would he keep on, pushing through my resistance until he came to the awful truth—I want him, badly. Even though I know that giving in to that wanting would be a disaster.

I sit down, take a cup of tea. It smells of flowers with a faint thread of smoke, and the taste is bright, robust. I suppose you could call this tea fortifying, like some British nurse in a World War II novel might.

Immediately I feel more awake, and I realize how tired I was before. I wake up at five each morning to go for a run and work out, which means I've been going nonstop for over fifteen hours now. My reaction to Cassian must have masked how worn out I am.

He pushes a plate toward me, which is piled high with sandwiches and sweets and slivers of fruit and melon.

"Thank you." I take the plate and choose one of the sandwiches, biting into it. It's roast beef with some kind of spicy, complex mustard on it. I can't help my little moan, because it's really good, especially as hungry as I am.

"You like it." Cassian's wearing a faint smile.

I swallow. "Lawford made this? It's amazing. It might be the best sandwich I've ever had. And really, a great sandwich is one of life's overlooked pleasures."

"I'll have to remember that."

Immediately I feel like an idiot. The women he usually dates probably aren't gushing over food as lowly as sandwiches. They probably eat only micro greens harvested by the light of a full moon sprinkled with cheese made from goats raised in someone's bedroom. If they eat at all.

But his gaze hasn't left my face, and he's watching me like he's waiting for my next reaction, my next noise of satisfaction.

I wet my dry lips, and his gaze follows that too.

"Don't stop," he says. "It was just getting good."

CHAPTER 4

She likes sandwiches. Loves them. And forgets to eat, she gets so focused on things.

It's all information that I meant to get out of her, the better to seduce her, but I wasn't expecting how her enjoyment would affect me. She bit into that sandwich, and the way she moaned... I'm going to dream about it tonight. Hell, I want to feed her from my own hand, the better to savor her reaction.

It's the first time she's let her guard down with me, eating that sandwich. And just like I predicted, she's soft, bubbly even, when she lets her shields down. Like a mouthful of the best champagne.

Which brings up the very intriguing idea of giving her some champagne. The bottles I have in my cellar are the finest, rarest stuff on earth. If a sandwich has her that worked up...

"Another sandwich?" I ask, pushing the tray toward her.

She looks at it regretfully. "I should finish what's on my plate first."

Ah, there's that discipline again. I bet she eats everything she's given even if she hates it.

"I won't tell anyone," I say. "If you want it, you should take it."

Another rule of seduction—although it's more of a technique—keep pushing a person toward what you know they want but they think they shouldn't have.

"But the rest of it might be just as good." She studies the plate. "I don't want it to go to waste."

"It won't. Trust me." I pick up another sandwich and hand it to her.

Her mouth flattens but she takes it. And then she's biting into it, her eyes fluttering closed as she does. "Oh, that's just as good as the last one. How does he do it?"

That tremor in her voice as she asks about Lawford has jealousy biting at my throat. And I don't get jealous. Life's too short to get hung up on one person.

"He can only make sandwiches," I say. "Can't cook anything else." I somehow manage to keep my tone light, uncaring.

"Oh." She finishes off the second sandwich. "I suppose when you make sandwiches like this, you don't need to know how to cook." She pauses with her fork reaching for a piece of melon. "You're not having anything."

"Because you're my entire focus here."

Another rule of mine: people love to be the center of attention. Even people who claim to hate the spotlight. If it's the right person giving them the attention, they'll eat it up. Which is another technique—making sure you're the right person.

She licks her lips again. Immediately my pulse picks up because she's done it twice now and she's never given herself away like that before. Which means I'm slowly getting my little tin soldier to come undone.

Then she blinks and the steel returns to her spine. "Shouldn't the computer be your focus?"

As if I can ever forget that ugly thing sitting between us. I'd rather focus on her—she's much more delightful.

But she's also right, unfortunately. Digging into that thing is more important at the moment.

I reach over and flick the rusty power switch. It moves slowly, reluctantly. "It wasn't supposed to be on." I'm not sure if I'm justifying it to her or myself.

"Then why put it in the car in the first place?" She's set her plate aside—her empty plate—and is leaning in, the full force of her attention on me.

"We thought it was ready for more intense testing." I stare at the metal box, remembering the hours of work we put into it. Running endless simulations, thinking up bigger and better ways to push the AI above and beyond. It wasn't like we wrote the software and thought our first attempt was awesome. We were constantly trying to see where it might fail, how we could improve it.

No, we didn't think our first attempt was awesome. But our thousandth or so attempt? Yeah, we did. And we thought it was almost ready for the real world.

We were wrong, and Ira and Tynan paid for it.

"What was Tynan like?" Victoria asks.

That was the last question I expected from her. Maybe more about what role I played, why I did it, what I planned to do about it now. But not Tynan.

My heart seizes with something deeper than shock. "He was… He had no one. Just came into life with no entanglements. It fascinated me."

People's entanglements are things you can play upon to manipulate their behavior, like a spider jiggling a strand of its web. Only less sinister. I always study what's important to people, what they're caught up in, because it tells me everything I need to know about the kind of message they'll respond to.

Tynan was a blank slate in many ways. Meeting him was

kind of like a biologist stumbling into the icy desert of Antarctica and wondering *What can possibly thrive here?*

And then we became friends. Closer than brothers. I suppose I became Tynan's entanglement, along with the rest of the guys. And we killed him. Possibly.

"That's all?" Victoria's expression shows faint distaste. "He had no family, and that's what you liked about him?"

My own expression hardens before I can catch it. "I didn't say that was the only thing."

"It was the *first* thing you thought of. Must have made it convenient when he disappeared—no one to come to you guys, demanding answers."

Jesus, she's like an avenging angel—no give, no mercy, just divine, unbending judgment. My little tin soldier would never do what I did, not in a million years. Death before dishonor.

"There was still Raven and Morgan and Oscar," I say coolly. "Which is why we didn't tell them."

At least until today, when we confessed everything. And broke everything, just as we feared. Raven will probably forgive us one day, but she won't forget. I don't know that Morgan will do either.

"You should have," Victoria says, as if it was just that easy. It probably would be for her.

"Not all of us can be as upstanding as you are," I drawl. I drape my arm over the back of my chair. She follows the motion with reluctant intensity. "Some of us were meant to be bad. But that's what you want, right? Someone to break your heart?"

She shakes her head, more strands escaping her ponytail. "No. No, the point is to keep that from happening." Desperation makes her tone splinter.

"Don't worry," I say mockingly. "You know how terrible I am; there's no danger of you falling for me, right? After all, I've killed men."

Her mouth flattens. "But you could be innocent. That's why we're working on this computer."

I put on a bitter smile. "I'm not. You saw the power switch. It was on, controlling the car when it went off the road. I'm guilty as hell."

"Then why do this?" Her brow is tight with frustration. Poor, honorable little thing—she doesn't understand twisted, not like me. She'd be hell to sell something to, she's so straight and narrow. "If you already think you're guilty, what's the point?"

"Because Tynan is trying to tell us something. Maybe he's telling us he blames us and he's going to have his revenge. In which case, I deserve it. Or maybe he's trying to tell us something else. In which case, I want to know."

Her eyes widen. "He could be coming to kill you."

I shrug. "Could be."

"So you're just going to let him?"

I bark out a laugh. "Oh no. What, you think I'm that self-sacrificing? No, if and when he comes, I'm going to fight. Deep down, I'm still that much of a selfish bastard."

"And the rest of them? Will they deserve it?"

I suppose to an outsider they would. We all worked together on this, each of us contributing our own unique skills to it. It never would have worked if even one of us was missing from the team. In a way, even Tynan is responsible for what happened.

So yeah, we do each deserve it. But Tynan sent this specifically to me. He pulled it out of the car as it began to sink, with Ira dead in the driver's seat, and kept it and himself hidden for five years... and then he put it on my desk not even a day ago.

"It's mine." I put a hand on the metal casing. It soaks up the heat from my palm. "Tynan made it mine when he put it in my office. And I don't give up what's mine."

Her lips part as she inhales. If I cup her jaw right now,

will my palm feel cool from the metal? Will she shiver at my touch?

"You never finished telling me about him."

I pull my hand back. "Tynan was the glue out of all of us. He didn't talk much, not as much as I do, and he didn't try to take charge like Gideon or glower us into submission like Gage. He brought us all into coherence. And he had a wicked sense of humor. Dark, supersarcastic. Drier than bones in a desert."

"Kind of like your sense of humor."

I shake my head. "No, I'm laughing at myself more than anything. It was different with Tynan. No one ever got pissed at his jokes."

"You want people to get pissed though."

I shrug because it's true and I don't really care that it's true. Humor's just another weapon when it comes down to it. Only an idiot would throw away a perfectly good weapon. "I was the one who was supposed to be accounting for human behavior, human error. But Tynan had this way of making the AI…" I search for the word I want. "*Nimble.* Machines don't act like humans—they're totally linear, no chaos in them. But he could program it to make leaps of logic. To jump from *A* to *P* in a way a person might. The way a computer shouldn't."

She narrows her eyes. "Chaos?" It's clear she does not like that notion. "But you don't want chaos in a self-driving car."

I laugh sharply. "But you've got it already, because you've got people on the road. Humans are the biggest form of chaos ever, and they're all steering thousand-pound death machines. If it was only computers driving, then yeah, self-driving cars would be simple."

"You sound like you like irrationality." Victoria gets that out through a tight jaw.

"I do. It's how I made my money—seizing on people's whims, their spur-of-the-moment decisions. No one really needs the things I advertise. But once you see my marketing campaign, you want it. You wonder how you ever lived without it."

"Is that what you do when you seduce someone? You're just selling sex?"

For a moment I'm caught speechless by the bitterness in her tone. But only for a moment. "Just sex?" I raise a challenging eyebrow. "Sex should never be *just* anything. When I'm seducing a woman, my entire focus is on her. Her needs, her wants, her most minute reactions. And that doesn't end the moment we reach the bed. It only intensifies."

She's looking at me like that can't possibly be true. And somewhere deep inside her, she desperately wants it to be.

"Jesus," I burst out. "What kind of assholes were you with before?"

CHAPTER 5

I sit up too fast, heat racing to my cheeks. I force it back by thinking of ice, of snow, of my cold, clear plan to never deal with a man like those previous assholes again.

"That's the point," I say with edged precision. "You're here to teach me to stay away from men like that. And you." I reach for the computer on the table. Unwittingly, I touch the spot where his hand was, surprised by the warmth that lingers there. "And I'm here to help you with this. Since we're done eating, we should get started."

He looks as if he'd like to argue, his too-sensual mouth flattening for a moment. But then he rises and takes the box from me. "The workshop is this way."

"You have a workshop?" I ask as I follow him. There's no sign of Lawford as we move through the halls. It's only the two of us.

"I do actually get my hands dirty from time to time," he says with practiced casualness. As if he doesn't care what I think about him.

"I would think you'd have that at the office. Not that you'd have one here at home."

He turns into another hallway, taking us past a library and a home gym. I recognize the gym from his Instagram, but not the library. "The workshop at the office is for everyone at work. This one is just for me."

We stop before a heavy metal door unlike any other I've seen in the house. A control panel is set into the wall, powering up when Cassian approaches it. He sets his free hand on the screen and the scanner gets to work.

"Welcome," a soft, androgynous voice says. There's a weighty clunk as the door bolt releases.

"Fort Knox would be jealous," I murmur.

Of course Cassian hears. He snorts. "This is the latest from Gage's company. The NSA would love to have this, although they're probably working on ordering it from him right now."

"You don't know for sure?" I follow him into the darkened room.

Lights snap on as he hits the threshold. "No. Gage keeps his client list very, very secret. As a security company should."

I catch my breath as I take in the space. This isn't a workshop—this is an amazingly high-end lab with the kind of toys I could only dream about when I was in the Signal Corps. He wasn't joking about getting his hands dirty. Although he was, in a way. This is so new and sleek and gleaming it makes my teeth hurt.

Cassian shuts the door firmly behind him. I can't help my surprised inhale as he locks us inside.

"To keep the cats out," he says. "The security is mostly for them."

I doubt that. Cassian sets the metal box on a table with several o-scopes and multimeters and computers already on it. Along with an ordinary-looking lab notebook.

My eyes go wide. "Is that... Is that one of the infamous notebooks?"

Cassian nods without looking away from the car-control computer. "You can look through it if you want." He laughs without humor. "If you can figure out what it says, then you'll be the hero of the hour. Or the decade."

I flip through it, seeing for the first time the thing that started this whole situation. Nothing about the words or equations makes sense to me because it's all in code. A code no one's been able to break.

See, Ira gave all six of his... adopted boys, I guess you'd call them, these notebooks in his will. Since Tynan was dead and had no family, Gideon—as the executor of the will—kept Tynan's notebook. None of them could figure out the code, and it sounds like after Ira's death, they were too shook up—and guilty—to really try.

So the notebooks sat for five years. Gideon kept his and Tynan's in a super-high-end safe, although again only because he felt guilty and not because he really thought someone would try to take it.

Until someone did try.

A woman broke into Gideon's amazingly well-protected house and tried to steal it. So Gideon called in Tess, my boss and friend, to put in a new security system. To skip to the end, Gideon and Tess are now together, Gideon gave Tynan's notebook to the thief—because Tynan might be alive—Archer is trying to decode the notebooks, and I'm here with Cassian trying to figure out exactly what happened when Ira's car crashed all those years ago.

Oh, and Ira has two daughters, Raven and Morgan, who didn't get notebooks. And Morgan actually designs the kind of computers we're about to take apart, for a car company called Inspiron.

I'm still not sure I have a handle on everything that's happened and who did what and who's related to who. So I'm going to focus on the task—and the man—in front of me.

I flip to the end of the notebook, which isn't any more understandable than the beginning. "It's like someone took a physics textbook and ran it through a simple encryption program and this is what came out."

Cassian has a screwdriver in his hand and is working on opening up the box. His brow is furrowed in this expression of concentration that makes my pulse go fluttery. I squash that sensation harder than a spider.

"If that were the case," Cassian says, "we would have decoded it by now. Ira used to give us puzzles like that." His hands still for a moment. "We thought those notebooks were just one last puzzle."

Which explains why none of them tried to solve them, not in any serious sense. A last gift from a man they thought they killed? No way were they touching them.

I shut the notebook. "I'm no good at puzzles. But I can help with the hardware."

I study the metal box more closely. Once again, I'm struck by how little rust there is. Lightly I touch some scratch marks at the edges. Those must have come from someone prying it out of the car. Probably in a panic.

"Have you tried to power it up?" I ask. Even a short dunk in the ocean might have corrupted the interior components beyond repair. And then we'd be screwed. After my tours overseas, I discovered just how fragile electronics really were. Extreme environments do a number on them.

Cassian shakes his head, moving to another screw. "I wanted to open it up and see how bad things were inside. You get to be here for the big moment."

Somehow the thought makes me nervous, my palms going sweaty. If it doesn't work, I shouldn't be surprised, and it really isn't my responsibility, but I'm still anxious. I suppose that's my curse, to always care about things that don't need me to care about them.

"I hope it works."

"You and me both, V—Victoria."

He makes my name dance out of his mouth. But I ignore

how that feels and pounce on his misstep. Cassian never flubs anything, but he just flubbed my name. I narrow my eyes. "Were you about to call me Vicky?"

I don't do nicknames. Not at all. And plus I have a cousin, an awful, annoying brat, who used to call me that just to wind me up. My spine stiffens and my teeth clench as I remember.

"No, you're not a Vicky. Not at all." He works on another screw, his fingers long and graceful as he patiently tries to get it to move. Most guys would have stripped the screw by now with their macho urgency. "But Victoria is a mouthful."

He sends me a look that makes me want to melt as I imagine him saying my name with his face between my thighs, breathing all those syllables into my most sensitive flesh.

I try to swallow and clear my throat at the same time, which causes a painful traffic jam there. "Um, I never minded Victoria."

"Oh, you're definitely a Victoria. At least most of the time." Slowly the screw begins to release. But Cassian doesn't rush it. "But sometimes I think you might…"

The assessing look he gives me has new, sharp heat rushing through me, pulling my nipples to painful points. He's hardly even touched me and I'm coming undone with only his words and looks. And in only a few hours.

"Might what?" I get out. I wet my lips, tasting my own mouth.

He sets down the screw and the screwdriver. "You might be a V. Just… V."

I frown. "V?" It sounds sharp, because it is, a dagger aimed at everything below it.

"Yep. Because you have to bite your lip—just the littlest bit—to say it." He demonstrates, and the sight of his teeth gripping his lower lip, oh so gently, makes my core flood with urgent need.

I test it out myself. His gaze is locked on my mouth, as intense as if he could devour my lips with only his eyes. I feel that attention of his on me as sharply as I feel my own teeth, sinking ever so slightly into the plumpness of my lip. "V," I breathe out as soft and serious as a caress.

"Exactly." Cassian doesn't move, although I want him to. I want him to put his mouth where I had my teeth. I want it so badly I might start to shake.

And then I remember that this is the plan. That none of this is spontaneous or real—that this is exactly what I asked for. A demonstration.

It's like a bucket of ice water dumps down my back. I sit up, snap up really, putting as much space between us as I can. Nicknames are probably rule number whatever on how to build intimacy with your target. A special nickname that no one else can use.

And I almost fell for it.

"I don't do nicknames," I say coolly. "So please don't call me that."

For a moment he looks almost upset. Like I've rejected a gift of his. But then before I can see it clearly, the expression vanishes and he's back to his usual smug imperturbability. "Okay. No nicknames."

He makes it sound like I said no orgasms. Which is probably another rule I should set down.

Although… if he can get me this worked up over a single letter in the alphabet, what can he do when he gets my clothes off?

I'm afraid to find out. And at the same time, I want to. Desperately.

CHAPTER 6

I knew it wouldn't be easy getting Victoria to unwind. But goddamn am I still frustrated with how quickly she shut down after telling me no nicknames.

She was into it, I'm certain of it. The way she tried it out, biting her lip harder than she needed to? I'm getting hard just thinking about it.

Which is a problem since I'm about to remove the last panel on the computer. Slowly I pull the metal sheet away from the brackets, trying not to anticipate what I'll see inside. Most likely, the components are ruined.

But when I get a look, I suck in air. It looks almost pristine. There's not even any dust, which I'd expect after it sitting somewhere for years.

"Tynan's already turned this on," I say, setting the metal cover aside. "Very recently too."

Victoria nods. "It's clean as a whistle. But that doesn't mean it works. Only that someone cleaned it out. And that it must not have touched the seawater at all."

I set my hands on the edge of the metal case. "The car was never found. They sent divers down, but there was nothing. And Ira—" My voice catches hard, but I force it forward. "He washed up on the beach. So maybe the car was never in the water?"

Victoria looks pale. "I don't know that it's any use trying to reconstruct that from what we see here."

Gratitude flows through me, because I don't want to force myself to think that through anymore. The circuits themselves are relatively safe. The circumstances that got them here though…

"Right." I clear my throat. "We should see what this can still do."

I search for the power outlet before remembering that it doesn't have a normal power cord because it was supposed to draw power from the car's electrical system. That's going to be a problem unless I can splice something up real quick.

Victoria is peering into the case and frowning. "This is… None of this fits together. That's from like ten years ago and that's— Is that melted?"

I glance at it. "Only part of it, and not the important part."

She shakes her head. "I feel like I'm going to find spit and baling wire holding something important together here."

"Everything had to be salvaged from somewhere else. But it all works. Or at least it did once."

She follows a connection from one chip to another. "I thought Ira was wealthy. Why did you have to use scraps? This looks like something we'd jury-rig out in the field."

"Ira thought we'd value it more if we had to work for the parts. Use our brains to figure out what could fit where instead of just ordering up everything we wanted. He figured we'd learn more, and he was right." Something about the sight of all that mismatched stuff is making my throat hurt. Like it's hard to look at.

So I look at Victoria. Her ponytail is falling over one shoulder, and she's got the sexiest look of concentration on her face. She's determined to figure this mess out.

"I don't even know where to start," she says. "And that's unusual for me."

"Wait." I go over to one of the desktop machines and wake it. "We made a wiring diagram. That should help."

"What about the software to test it? Do you still have that?"

"I do." A few clicks take me into our original archives, the ones we haven't touched since Ira died. "Shit. Some of this stuff is really out of date. We might need to dig out some old compilers too."

"Or how about we build a time machine and go back five years to use that technology?"

I freeze without meaning to. If I could go back five years…

Victoria claps her hand over her mouth, her eyes going wide with horror. "I'm so sorry. I wasn't thinking. I never should have said that."

"It's okay," I say gruffly. "I know it was my fault. I'm not shrinking away from that."

"Still, I shouldn't have said it." She's rigid in her apology, as if mentally berating herself. "I was wrong."

There's something so… so damn touching about the way she said it. Formal and at attention, probably just like she did back when she was an officer.

"It's fine." I push the computer case out of reach. "And you're right—we'll need some supplies before we can get this running. I'll make a list and get some people on it."

She looks longingly at the machine. "So we can't do anything with it tonight?"

Immediately I consider a thousand more enjoyable things we can do besides tear apart my past. A lot of them involve me whispering "V" into her ear and watching her shudder, and even more involve her screaming my name with pleasure.

"Besides go through the wiring diagrams? No." I take in

her expression and sigh. "But we can definitely do that at least."

I turn the monitor so that we can both see the circuit diagram I pulled up. It's the main one and doesn't go into detail about the individual chips we put into the machine. What we built here was a thinking machine—you can't capture all that in a simple 2-D rendering.

Victoria studies the monitor, finding each component, then searching it out inside the case, giving this little nod of satisfaction when she locates it. Her lips move almost imperceptibly, as if she's speaking the logic of the circuits into her memory. Not once does she stop to ask me to clarify anything or what some component does.

"You know a lot about electronics," I say. Certainly I wasn't expecting someone who works for a small security system company to catch on so quickly.

"I majored in electrical engineering," she says distractedly. "With a minor in cybersecurity, although some of that is already outdated."

"You went to West Point."

She goes rigid. "Yes. I did." For a moment she looks as if she's staring off at something awful. Then, with effort, she goes back to studying the circuits.

"Bad memories?" I ask quietly. The military academy certainly left its stamp on her, but I can't imagine coming out of it was easy.

She inhales deeply. "It's not what you think. What does this chip do?" Her long index finger hovers over a chip.

It's an abrupt and clumsy change of subject, but I let it go. "That's mine." I smile at her surprise. "That's the chip I designed to account for the other cars—the other humans—on the road. This"—I point out another chip—"processes the features of the road. Buildings, billboards, curbs—Jesus, was it hard to get it to recognize curbs—animals, landscaping. It had to identify what was *road*—features it had to care about

—and what wasn't *road,* which it couldn't quite ignore and had to be ready to react to."

She's watching me with rapt attention. "Who programmed that?"

"Bishop. The trick was in the training data he fed it."

Her gaze falls on the other chip. "But you designed that."

I did. The feelings that little chip inspires in me… When I finished it, I thought it was my greatest achievement. And when Ira died, it felt like a curse. And now…

"Once the computer decides what is road and not road," I say, "it needs to watch and predict the behavior of the other cars so it can respond appropriately. Basically, it needs to read the other drivers' minds."

"I can't even read other people's minds."

I shake my head. "But you do every day. You see the nonverbal cues they give, and you predict their emotional state, their future reactions, based on those. It's the same in a car. Close your eyes."

She resists of course, widening her eyes before asking, "Why?"

"A thought experiment." I lower my voice. "Just trust me. Close your eyes."

When she does, relieved triumph surges through me. Her chin is tipped forward slightly, her lips are parted—she looks like she's waiting for a kiss. But she's skeptical about it; the line between her brows says that. I'd like to kiss that skepticism away.

Instead, I talk about four-way stops. "Imagine you're driving."

"What am I driving?"

I almost laugh, because of course she'd want to be precise about her own fantasy. "What do you want to be driving? Any car in the world, you could be driving it."

She has to think about it a moment. "A Mini Cooper." As soon as it comes out of her mouth, her cheeks go pink. She's embarrassed by her fantasy car. Probably because she doesn't believe she should be zipping around in something small and cute.

She's not small—her mouth would land right on my chin if we were face-to-face—and she's not cute. She's fucking gorgeous. And I'm beginning to think that her old boyfriends should be horsewhipped for not appreciating her.

"Good choice," I say in a low voice. The color in her cheeks deepens and shifts into something closer to desire. "Now, you're driving along, windows down, hair blowing in the breeze."

"My hair is never down."

"It is for this. Now, you're in your— What color is it?"

"I don't know what colors they come in."

I can only stare at her for a moment. "Let's not worry about that."

She almost cracks one eye open.

"Keep them closed," I say. "Now pick a color. Any color. It doesn't even have to be a real color."

"How…?" She closes her mouth and sighs, determination crinkling her nose. "Okay, any color. And my hair is down. Maybe… purple, like the sky at sunset. Just before it goes to black."

"Perfect. So your hair is down, you're cruising in your deep purple Mini Cooper and—"

Her hands flex on the table with frustration. "I don't understand the point of this."

"Patience. We need the setup before we reach the climax. Foreplay, if you like." Before she can say anything, I go on. "You come to a four-way stop."

"Is anyone else there? Or coming?" She lifts her head, turning it to the right and left as if looking for those imaginary cars.

"Yes. Another car comes to the stop sign at the exact same

moment you do. You make a complete and full stop, of course."

A ghost of a smile glimmers on her lips. "Rolling stops are very dangerous. Is this person to my right or left?"

"I can't tell you. You have to decide who goes first based solely on nonverbal cues."

She frowns. "Do they wave me through?"

"No."

"Then I wave them through."

"Nope, can't do that."

Her mouth turns down. "Do they come to a complete stop?"

"Yes. You're both sitting there at a dead stop, waiting for the other to move."

She's so serious as she imagines this it makes my heart twist in a strange way. This isn't a lark to her even though it's completely fake. "They're not moving at all?"

I can give her the hint of a lifeline here, but I won't. "No. So who goes first? The car has to figure it out. How would you figure it out?"

She may not know this consciously, but there are cues that tell you. And an unspoken hierarchy of who goes first. Yes, the law says the person to the right goes first, but some people forget that when they come to a stop sign. It's all about the unspoken rules of human behavior.

"Is the other driver a man?"

Ah, now she's getting down to the more relevant aspects. "You can't tell. And neither can the computer."

Her mouth purses. "How close to the line at the stop sign is he? Or she? Or they?"

Another great question. People who stop close generally weren't wanting to stop at all. And will be the first ones through. But that's too easy. "Same distance as you are."

Her eyes snap open, the green of them bright with accusation. "You're purposefully making this hard!"

"You've never been in this exact situation many, many times?" I keep my tone cool, quiet. "And yet somehow you decided who would go first and aren't still sitting at that stop sign."

"I wait a moment to see if they'll go first." She tosses that out defiantly. Looks like I managed to burrow under the ice princess's shell.

"You wait. They don't go. So you do. And at the same time, they go too."

She growls, probably the same way she would if she were really in this situation. "I'm out farther. I'm going."

"Taking charge?"

"Someone has to."

Of course—that's what she's been trained for. You don't go to West Point to come out a follower. Which makes me wonder all over again why she's not still in the Army, being a real-life Captain America.

"Now," I ask, "how do you get a computer to decipher that entire interaction? How do you have a machine understand people being people?"

Her expression falls. "I don't know. Sometimes I think I don't even understand people being people."

Which is where I come in. I'm supposed to teach her how to avoid people like me. To read our cues and run like hell when she sees them. My mouth floods with a sour taste. "Look, it's not you—"

My phone suddenly buzzes with a message. It's from Gideon. *What have you done with Victoria? She was supposed to call Tess when she got home, and Tess is freaking out.*

"Is everything okay?" Victoria asks.

I start to type out a reply. "It's fine. Gideon just thinks I've abducted you."

"Oh." She puts her hand to her mouth. "I forgot to text Tess. I told her I would when I got home." She frowns. "What are you saying to Gideon?"

I hit Send. "I told him that I kidnapped you. That I've locked you in my bedroom and you're never coming out. And that he can't say shit because he did the same to Tess."

Her cheeks go pink. For such a tightly wound woman, she sure does blush a lot. "Please don't tell him that. I'm messaging Tess right now."

"Too late." My phone buzzes again—Gideon's angry reply pops up on the screen. "Oh look, he's demanding I release you immediately. I don't think I will."

Victoria glances up from her own phone. "Is that what you're telling him?" She shakes her head. "Clearly I am not a prisoner. And…" She stops typing. "Well, I can't explain it to *them*, but we have an agreement."

"Why can't you tell Tess?" I wasn't planning on telling Gideon, but I'm curious why Victoria won't tell Tess.

"It looks…" She starts typing again, slower this time. "It looks bad. I'm using you to teach me how to avoid men. I should be able to figure this out on my own. I mean, Tess is great at finding nice guys."

I can't help but bust out laughing. "You think Gideon is nice? You think I'm an asshole but he's nice?" I'm also a touch offended, because Gideon really did hold Tess hostage—kind of—and I'm going along with this scheme Victoria is too embarrassed to tell anyone about.

"Gideon was a departure for her." She sets the phone down. "I told Tess I was on my way home."

There's a challenge in her eyes. Like she might be daring me to keep her here. Or at least to suggest it.

I decide to surprise her instead and be the perfect gentleman. "Of course. Let's get you home."

Before she can drop her gaze, I catch the flash of disappointment. Excellent. Exactly the reaction I wanted. But I keep my smile bland.

There's time to push her again. And I plan to do it very soon.

CHAPTER 7

"Oh wow, you made so much progress with him!"

I watch as Jacinda, one of the teenagers who comes to work with the dogs, leads Fido, a feisty terrier, from one end of the yard at the shelter to the other. Fido trots happily, proudly, at her side, the leash between them slack.

"He doesn't pull at all anymore," the girl says. "I don't even have to tug him to get him going."

"Your patience paid off." I bend down and give Fido's ears a rub. "And just in time; someone wants to come see him next week."

Jacinda's smile dims a fraction. "Really? It's good, since he's been here so long…"

"But you'll miss him." I straighten up. "I will too."

When I first thought of starting this program, I agonized over it. Would working with dogs looking for forever homes remind the kids too much of their own situations? Would it simply be too painful?

For some kids, it is. They come to the program and find it's not for them. But other kids, like Jacinda, flourish. It's hard to say goodbye to the pups, but it also reminds them that as powerless as they might feel, they can help the dogs, and one day they'll be back with their own families.

I won't deny we had a few disasters at the beginning. When I started the Instagram, I made sure to only show the adoptable dogs and to refer to the kids very obliquely to protect their privacy. But I still got a wave of people wanting to know how they could adopt the kids or kids *and* the dogs, as if the program was a one-stop shop for an instant suburban family.

So now the Instagram is only about the dogs, and I'm careful to never reveal our meeting locations, and only a few people at the shelter know that it's foster kids coming every Saturday to help with the dogs.

Jacinda scans the yard filled with dogs and kids. Everyone's supposed to be working, either on a simple obedience command or playing with their dogs. The playing is going better than the obedience. "I see Hugo's here, but he's not working with Duke."

"Duke's off on a family visit," I say. "A really nice couple with a yard and no other dogs."

Jacinda nods approvingly. She knows dogs incredibly well—once she's older, I can see her running the shelter. "And kids?"

"No kids."

Her mouth flattens. "Too bad. He was good with kids. But he'll probably get spoiled, become their dog kid." She motions toward Hugo with her chin. "He know yet?"

"I told him. He understands, and he was excited to start with Dolly." I check my watch. "Oh shoot, we've got to start cleaning up."

Before I can do anything, Jacinda puts two fingers in her mouth and lets out a long whistle. "Time to put everything away."

It's so much like having a great sergeant by my side again I almost smile. But it's tinged with bitter sweetness.

"Thanks," I tell Jacinda, my voice only a little husky. And then I help the kids put the dogs away, clean up the toys and the leashes, clean up the messes the dogs left, and say goodbye as the kids are picked up one by one. By the time it's over, I'm ready to lie on the couch for the rest of the day.

And then my phone buzzes. A message from Cassian.

Immediately my body comes awake, my skin tingling with adrenaline. He dropped me off at home two days ago, saying goodbye without even trying to steal a kiss or make another date for us to meet. And then he left me hanging.

I wasn't angry, because I figured that was one of his tricks. Have all those intimate moments at his house, then cut me off completely for a few days. Make me desperate for his presence.

Well, it didn't work. I was a touch anxious, but only because I couldn't work on the car AI. It's important to figure out what's going with it as soon as we can.

So that's why my heart is racing as I open his message. Because I want to get into the guts of that computer. His lessons aren't more important as that. I'm not planning on dating anyone anytime soon. At least not until I've learned everything I can from him.

Dinner. Tonight. I'll pick you up at seven.

I don't even consider telling him I'm busy or tell him off for arranging this without even asking me. I'm too keyed up at the thought of seeing him again. Which is bad, but he's going to teach me to not be this way.

Sure. That's a good reply—casual, uncaring. Not as tentative as okay, not exactly enthusiastic. I can take it or leave— Oh God, I'm massively overthinking this.

But I can't shake the sense of tingling anticipation, and I'm still obsessing over what we might be doing tonight when I meet Tess for lunch. We're at our favorite dim sum place in the Richmond, tucking into the most amazing pork buns.

"So, how are things going with Cassian?" Tess asks casually, but I still tense up. Even though I was expecting this exact question.

She means on the car AI, but I can't help but think about him taking me on a date tonight, trying his damnedest to seduce me. Cassian is a world-class playboy, and I'm about to get the full force of his charm. Or will he only use half power on me? At least at first?

"Um." I put down my chopsticks. "It's… it's kind of haphazardly put together. I mean, one chip was even half-melted. Cassian said he'd need to get some parts before we can fire it up. But I did see the wiring diagram, and I've been studying that."

I was up way too late last night looking at it actually, trying to tease out the logic of what they built. It's so intricate, even for something cobbled together five years ago with spare parts. I can see the hints of genius in it already.

I've also gotten way too obsessive about the dynamics of four-way stops. Every time I came to one today, I spent way too long thinking about who was supposed to go when and how I instinctively knew when it was my turn. Cassian would have died laughing watching me.

"Gideon said Cassian had to even order some cables from some lab in Russia," Tess says. Her gaze goes a touch dreamy at the mention of Gideon, as it always does.

I'm torn between happiness for her and worry. Tess has felt like my responsibility since she was assigned to my unit all those years ago, especially with what happened with her harasser and how I couldn't stop him. We might be just civilians now, but I'll always carry that weight with me.

When she took the job with Gideon and agreed to his insane terms, I lost my mind, although outwardly I was mostly supportive. And when she fell for him, I really lost it, although again, I didn't show it.

Gideon isn't anything like the guys Tess dated before—he's wealthy, insists on getting his own way, and he's caught in the same dark situation Cassian is. But none of the guys Tess dated before could put that look on her face. And I'm happy that she's happy like this.

So I'm keeping my worry to myself. "What does Gideon think of all this?" I ask, picking up my chopsticks again. "Cassian said some stuff about how it might mean Tynan is looking for revenge. And he seemed very fine about that."

Tess's eyebrows shoot up. "I don't think Gideon is fine with that. Although he is concerned about what Tynan—if he's alive—is up to with all this." She lowers her voice. "Have you noticed that Cassian is kind of… nihilistic?"

I frown without even thinking about it, because it's not that Cassian doesn't care. When he was talking about deserving it from Tynan, that was pretty far from not caring. And he's definitely passionate about studying human behavior even if I don't agree with how he applies that information.

I force myself to relax because it's not my job to defend him. "I don't know about that." I reach for another pork bun. "I couldn't say though."

Tess tilts her head. "But you will be able to. After you're done working with him on the AI. Why did you volunteer for that? I didn't think you liked him."

Tess is understating things—she knows I heartily dislike Cassian. Or at least I did. "It's one of the very first self-driving cars, and they built it all themselves. And it might have killed someone. So of course I'm curious." The butter-flies in my stomach flutter madly, reminding me of every-thing I'm leaving out. But no matter how much I love Tess, I can't admit to her that I've contracted Cassian to teach me how to deal with men. To teach me how to keep my heart from getting broken.

"Well, if he gets to be too much for you," she says, "tell me and I'll let Gideon know. One of the guys can help Cassian. It's funny, but when you didn't text right away to say you'd gotten home after you left with him, I got so worried. I kept imagining him…"

I raise my eyebrows. "Kidnapping me and forcing me to do the work entirely under his supervision, twenty-four seven?"

Tess clears her throat even as she tries to hide a smile. "Yeah. I mean, it worked out for me, but I wouldn't want it to happen to you. The hostage-taking part. But falling in love…" Her smile widens and goes dreamy.

"There's no danger of either of those," I say dryly.

If Tess hears the hint of bitterness in that, she doesn't let on. And I'm glad, because really, I don't want to be mopey about my love life and jealous that Tess is so happy. I'm taking charge of this with my lessons with Cassian. Everything with men will be different after that. Better. Happier.

"Anyway." Tess blinks hard like she's waking herself up. "We're talking about you. And Cassian. So, when are you getting back to work on the car computer?"

Tonight? Maybe? I have no idea if Cassian intends to do any actual work tonight or if this is fake-date time only. I should have asked that. My fevered brain just went straight to date and…

"I have nothing to wear." My veins go cold as ice water as I realize how mediocre my closet is. If we're only working, I'm fine. I've got plenty of work wear. But date wear? Oh hell. I don't think business casual is going to cut it. Or even business formal.

"Nothing to wear where?" Tess is deeply concerned, probably because I don't usually send the conversation veering into an odd direction like a drunk at the wheel. "Is everything okay? You… I'm not saying this to be mean, but you've been a little distracted today. And that's not like you at all."

She's right. I'm usually a better friend than this. But I'm

keeping secrets and being ashamed of something I'm doing… That's not me.

"Cassian's teaching me how to avoid men like him," I blurt out before I can lose my nerve. Sometimes you just have to charge a fixed position and hope for the best. "It was part of our agreement to have me help him."

Tess is speechless. Her mouth is open, but nothing's coming out.

"Don't you dare feel sorry for me," I say quickly. "After what happened with Todd, I… This is me taking control. Those kinds of guys are bad for me. If I can avoid them, I'll find a guy who's good for me."

Tess chews on her bottom lip. "I wasn't going to feel sorry for you. And I guess if you want to find out a bad boy's secrets, Cassian is the perfect person to go to. He's like the alpha bad boy. Have you seen his latest Instagram post?"

"Do I want to?" But of course I do. I stalk his feed like an addict looking for her next fix. Although I haven't looked yet today—maybe exposure to the man himself has cured my addiction.

Tess hands over her phone. There's Cassian, in all his lazy, beautiful glory, sprawled in a leather chair, half a day's stubble on his face. His crisp white shirt is mostly unbuttoned, like we caught him undressing, and next to him is an upturned champagne flute, golden, fizzy liquid spilling in a pool on the floor.

The champagne glass is supposed to look like an accident, but it's all so painfully staged it makes my teeth hurt. And the comments underneath… One person even offered to personally lick up every drop of that champagne.

The caption is only one word: *Thirsty?*

Well, he certainly is. For attention.

I hand the phone back, my mouth a tight line. "It's certainly… something."

"Gideon said he's getting as bad as Axel Beck."

Axel Beck is the CEO of Inspiron, probably the most successful electric-car company in the world. Morgan works there, designing AI for cars, and is dating Axel. Axel's Instagram is justifiably famous—he looks like a model and isn't afraid to flaunt it.

Cassian is even more devastatingly handsome, but he can't be mistaken for a model. His smile is way too knowing. Not bland enough. His smile promises that he's dangerous.

Tess puts the phone away. "So, he's… fake dating you? For instructive purposes?"

I shrug. "Yes. I guess. He told me to be ready for dinner tonight, but I didn't ask what for. Maybe we're only working."

Tess rolls her eyes. "No, you're not. A man like Cassian doesn't invite someone over for a working dinner. And yes, we should find you something to wear."

"I don't know…" Suddenly the thought of dressing up and taking this all very seriously is making my head spin. It can't be too real. If it's too real… I don't know what then, only that the thought is making my heart race way too fast.

"Yes," Tess says firmly. "Cassian's going to be pulling out all the stops—he's just as competitive as Gideon, and if he sees this as a challenge, which I'm sure he does—you're going to need armor."

Armor. Now that I can understand. And she's right; clothes are their own kind of armor. "Okay." I nod my head. "Okay," I say more firmly. "You're right. I'll need armor. Now where can we get some?"

Tess's smile is slow and wicked. "I know exactly where to go."

CHAPTER 8

"There's something missing from this." I tap the photograph in question, one of a dozen spread out on my desk. "The entire composition—the message—is off because of it."

My head of marketing peers at the picture; the photographer leaning in too. We've just finished a four-hour photo shoot, but I insisted on printing out and going over the shots immediately. I could have been easygoing and let everyone review them on the computer screen, do a few quick touch-ups in Photoshop, but I'm a hard-ass. I want pictures that look good from the start, and I can't see them all together properly on a screen.

Yes, it's a pain in the ass, but I didn't make my company the number one marketing firm in the world by cutting corners.

Kaya, my head of marketing, taps the corner of the shot. "It looks too… too sparse."

She's pointing to a photo of me in my office. These are all photos of me, all looking way too bored with how awesome my life is. Somehow we've crossed the line from effortless luxury to ennui.

I pinch the bridge of my nose. "These are all wrong."

Jax, the photographer, looks up in surprise. "How? It's not that different from the last set we did."

"I look like an asshole. In each and every one." My smile is dark, twisted. The kind of smile I usually keep to myself and don't show the entire world.

Kaya frowns. "You're right. You do."

Gideon would have torn her head off for that, but I foster more honesty and less cowering in my company.

Jax inhales sharply. "It's your face. Have you..." They glance nervously at me. "Have you had anything done recently?"

They mean fillers or plastic surgery. But what's really happened is that my past has come home to roost, bleak and black and murderous.

"No," I say shortly. "You're right—it is my face, but it's not because of any work I've had done." I gather up the pile and put them all in the trash.

Bruiser immediately jumps up on the desk, making Kaya and Jax lean as far away as they can. He's never scratched them, but just his size alone intimidates most people.

He blinks me at me as if to ask *Are you done with this?*

"Never mind," I say. "Post something from the other sessions on my personal Instagram this week. The ones that didn't pass."

I run everything I put on my social media through my own proprietary AI to determine exactly how people will engage with it—certain things get looked at longer, others get more comments or likes, others more shares. And some even increase sales. All of it is perfectly timed to make the exact impression I want it to.

"That will screw up the metrics for this latest campaign," Kaya says.

"I know. But it's better than putting me out looking like that."

Kaya and Jax exchange a look. Great, now I'm becoming

the crazy, unreasonable CEO. But they leave without saying anything more than "Okay."

As they're walking out, my assistant walks in, carrying a large padded shipping envelope. "You wanted me to give you this as soon as it came," she says, setting it on my desk.

"Thanks." When I see the return address, I wait for her to shut the door behind her before I open it.

It's the chips I had custom made, the final piece in getting the AI up and running again. With these in hand, Victoria and I can be working on it in a matter of hours.

Or I can take her for a private dinner at my club like I planned.

Exploring the dark secrets of my past or exploring the intense connection I have with a beautiful, intriguing woman? Yeah, that's not even a contest. Dinner is definitely happening.

I unlock my desk drawer and put the envelope in it, right on top of the computer case in there. Underneath the case is the notebook Ira left me. After everything that's happened, I'm keeping them close. They're never more than an arm's reach away from me.

Once I lock the drawer, I call up the internal Slack channel, intending to get my marketing team to send me the latest data on the campaign we're designing for Pixio. But my phone rings before I can.

I stare at the caller ID with a tight jaw. This is last call I want to take right now. But I have to. I always have to.

"Dad." I bite that out. He's not getting a better greeting from me.

He grunts. "Need to talk to you."

My stomach sinks even though I'm resolved to not let him get to me. I've been swearing that for years now, and it never seems to work. "What?"

"Your sister showed me that crap you put on the internet. You look ridiculous."

"That ridiculousness pays your mortgage," I say with so much politeness my teeth could crack. "Did you just call to tell me how disappointed you are or for something else? If it's something else, let's get to it. I get tired of a broken record."

Dad snorts. "You're still scamming people. Oh, you're a lot slicker at it now, but it's still scamming. Think I'm proud my son is famous for cheating people out of money?"

I've heard this all before, so many times. And yet my pulse surges with anger all the same. "I haven't run any scams for years. And that money I brought in? You called it dirty but took it all the same."

"We had all those bills!" His voice is rising, rising. "The hospital wanted to take the damn house, that's how much we owed. And still…" His voice stops as if something is choking him.

I already know what he was going to say. *And still Mom died.*

"You know what?" That's as sharp and short as my temper. "We're not talking about this again. If you want something else, get to it. Otherwise, I'm hanging up."

There's a moment where it sounds like he's getting ahold of himself. I don't let it touch me at all. He called me. He instigated this.

"The sink broke. The one in the guest bathroom. Flooded the whole cabinet."

I look toward the ceiling. Right. Something to fix. Because I'm my dad's landlord and have to take care of those things. I can pass it off to a management company or even my assistant, but I haven't. Maybe because some nasty part of me enjoys having him come to beg me for things.

"I'll send over someone today," I say. Finally my tone is completely neutral. "Is that all?"

"Yeah." He hangs up before I can.

For a moment I'm tempted to throw my phone against

the wall. But that won't make my dad magically better, won't make me into the kind of son he wanted, won't bring my mom back. It'll only break my phone. So I don't.

Instead, I call up Oscar. Oscar was Ira's best friend, and after Ira died, he kind of took Ira's place in our lives. Not completely, because no one can be Ira, but he was there if we wanted to talk. Gideon resented him for that while Bishop felt way too guilty to get close to Oscar. Gage… Gage doesn't talk to anyone, but Archer goes to Oscar occasionally for advice.

I'm pretty sure I talk to him the most. Yeah, I feel guilty, and Oscar offers me reassurance I'm not a complete piece of shit. That I still matter to someone. After all the crap I get from my dad, it's nice to have someone treat me like I'm not a huge disappointment. Not that I'd ever admit that to anyone. It'd be bad for my brand.

Bane takes the opportunity to slink into my office. He never comes around when other people are here, and he's somehow mastered the trick of walking through closed doors and walls, always appearing even when I have no idea how he got in.

Bruiser blinks down at him from the desk. Bane ignores him, taking the opportunity to groom his remaining ear with his paw. I've probably only pet Bane a dozen times since I adopted him—he never lets me get that close. Yet he sticks around anyway. I have no doubt the cat can escape the house if he wants to.

I suppose he's found something he needs here besides food. Which he eats plenty of, despite how skinny he is. I've had him checked for every possible disease, but he just naturally won't put on weight. It's like he's expecting to turn back into a street cat at any moment.

Oscar answers with a jovial, "Cassian! What's on your mind?"

I look away from my puzzling cat. "Not anything in particular. I was just feeling restless."

"You have enough free time to be restless?"

"No," I admit. "But I'm doing it anyway."

"Something bothering you?"

The deep resonance in Oscar's voice tugs at me, tempting me to tell him everything. But the warm concern would immediately leave if I told him I was responsible for the death of his best friend.

We told Raven and Morgan the truth, or at least that we suspected that we might be responsible. Raven took some time, but she decided to keep us in her life. And to help figure out exactly what happened. Morgan stopped talking to us for a while, but… well, she's talking to us again, and that's about it.

It was agreed that it was best to keep all this from Oscar. At his age and with his heart condition, hearing Ira's death might not have been an accident could have dire results. So I've been keeping on with Oscar as if nothing's changed.

"Just the usual," I say. "Keeping a massive company afloat and growing, coming up with ideas that are 'the same but different,' refining our AI even more… Typical stuff."

Oscar barks out a laugh. "Yeah, very usual for you. You know, Ira would be so proud of what you boys have done. Truly. I wish so badly he were here to see you."

"I—" Jesus, is my throat closing? I can talk to my own dad about my mother dying and not bat an eye, but Oscar mentions Ira and I'm ready to bawl. With effort, I shove all that into the pit of my stomach. "I wish he were here too."

"He'd have been so impressed with what you guys are doing with the AI." If Oscar hears my flash of emotion, he doesn't let on. "Compared to what we had, it's so advanced."

Ira was pretty well known for his early work on AI, bringing it from a solely theoretical application to something you could use in the real world. Oscar was his partner on that.

Once Ira died, Oscar never really worked in AI again. Maybe it was too painful after that to do the work without Ira, but I could never ask.

"You guys were doing advanced stuff too," I say. "Things we haven't even attempted."

Oscar and Ira were working on brain-machine interfaces, using programming to let computers talk to neurons and vice versa. Imagine controlling a computer solely through your thoughts—that was their dream. Their work was only in the initial stages when Ira died.

For obvious reasons, none of the guys have worked on anything like that at all. Guilt is a hell of a drug.

"Well…" Oscar lets that trail off into a nothingness filled with grief and regret. "How's Gideon doing? I hope he brings Tess back to dinner sometime."

"He's fine. And I'm sure he'll bring her to next Tuesday's dinner—they're pretty serious."

"Good, good. You going to bring anyone?" Oscar's tone is amused because he already expects me to say no. I always say no, and I've never brought anyone to meet the guys or Raven and Morgan and Oscar.

Victoria has already met most of them though. It wouldn't be so odd if I brought her.

Except that's not part of the playbook, introducing a woman to my closest friends. I'll make her pleasure my exclusive focus while we're together, but bringing her outside the bubble I've created for the two of us isn't happening. Victoria only wants to see me as a playboy, a bad boy, a ruiner of women. Not as anything else.

She's kind of like my dad when you put it like that.

"No," I say more shortly than I mean to. "You know that."

"Okay." Oscar clears his throat. "And how's the rest of them?"

We spent another few minutes talking about the guys, Morgan's latest trip with Axel to Chile, Raven's plans for an unbirthday celebration for Gage. Oscar doesn't seem to have noticed that the atmosphere between all of us is decidedly chillier. For him, everything is the same as it ever was as he discusses what's been going on. All ordinary stuff, but deep too. Intimate.

By the time I hang up, I already feel a thousand times better. Yeah, my dad thinks I'm a piece of shit, but Oscar doesn't. Although he should.

A glance at the clock tells me it's time to get ready for my date with Victoria. As I leave my office, I wonder: Am I proving to her how awful I really am with these lessons? Or am I hoping to prove to her that I'm really not?

I don't have an answer.

CHAPTER 9

This skirt might have been a mistake.

Tess is the one who found it tucked in the back of a rack at the store she took me to. It's a pencil skirt, which sounds boring, but not when it hugs my curves in slippery black satin. Then it's definitely not boring. Pairing it with a crisp white button-down shirt like I've done takes it to another level of sexy. I'm covered, but I feel like a sexpot all the same.

Cassian's gaze ran over me and lingered when he picked me up. I felt like flames were licking over my skin as he did.

"I like the skirt," he said, his voice low.

He kept glancing at my legs as he drove us to dinner, like he literally could not take his eyes off me. Like I was magnetized. It made me feel both alluring and anxious.

When we arrived at his club—his private club—we were whisked up to the roof garden where a table for two was set up amid lush greenery and looking out over a sparkling blue pool. And then beyond, the Bay Bridge glittered against the dark water.

I was completely captivated, walking toward the view without thinking. And then my skirt started to sneak up. And up. And up.

A pencil skirt isn't new to me—heck, my service uniform

had a pencil skirt. But a satin pencil skirt turned out to be a whole new beast.

So here I am, sitting at a table with the most compelling man I've ever met, one intent on showing me the best time ever, and my skirt won't stop being noticeable.

Each time I shift, it threatens to ride up my thighs. And when I pull it down, the fabric slides across my skin in the most arousing way.

I'm trying to concentrate on my food and the wine, but Cassian is so close I can smell his aftershave—something like citrus and fresh-cut wood—and I've got one hand on my skirt hem, my fingers pressing into the soft spot just above my knee.

I'm beyond addled—my skin flushed, my pulse erratic, my thoughts all of his scent. And how he looks. And how he moves. And how I wish it was his hand at my knee and not mine.

"What's wrong?" he asks in a low tone.

"Nothing." I shake my head as I tug at my hem. "What do you mean?"

"You've been pulling at your dress all night." He actually leans over the table to get a look. "Is something poking you?"

"No." I release my hem, but it's too late. He's already seen. "I'm fine."

He doesn't straighten up. "Is something wrong with your skirt? You can change if it's bothering you."

Into what? "It's not like I'm not used to wearing skirts." I hiss at him. "Or sexy clothes. Don't think that."

"I wasn't." He raises an eyebrow.

"It's just..." I reach for my hem again, then stop myself. "It's fine. This maybe wasn't the best choice."

"Why not? You said you're comfortable in it. You look damn sexy... What's the problem?"

The problem is him. He makes me feel... not that my skin is wrong, but that my skin is wrong when he's not touching it. That these clothes should be on the floor and not on me. And he didn't even have to really do anything to make me feel this way. He just turned his super sex ray on me or something.

"I usually wear more normal clothes on dates," I admit. "So maybe this was a mistake."

His smile is slow, knowing. "Let me tell you a little secret, Victoria. No matter what you wear, I'm still going to be insanely, wildly, maddeningly attracted to you. Any man who looks at you and sees your clothes first... Well, they're fucking blind."

My first instinct is to blurt *You're attracted to me?* But that would be silly, because of course he is. He just said it, and it's not like I'm repulsive. My next instinct is to answer my own question with *Of course he is, he's attracted to everyone,* but I'm not sure that's true. His focus is so intense on me I could wear only his gaze in a snowstorm and stay toasty warm.

But again, that's his special skill—to make someone feel like the center of his world. This is what I'm supposed to be learning to avoid, this feeling as if I'm special.

"Do you come up with this on the spot?" I ask with real curiosity. "Or do you practice a few things beforehand?"

Instantly his expression shutters. "You think I'm lying."

"No, not that," I assure him. "Just maybe... not complete honesty."

"You think I'm selling you something." His tone is so flat —it shouldn't have room for that much bitterness.

"That's your job."

His expression clears, goes bland again. "Exactly. Well, to answer your question, no, I didn't practice any of what I just said to you."

"That's not helping." I notice he didn't specify if he practices things he says to other women.

He throws up his hands. "It's not like I have a battle plan. I see a woman I'm attracted to, I ask if she'd like to go out. I find something I think she'll enjoy. I make sure her enjoyment is my entire focus. And that's it. I don't have any magic spells or hookup-artist tricks or anything like that. I'm just me. Lying, conniving, scamming Cassian."

I blink at him, unable to find anything to say. "I never..." But I did kind of call him a scammer. A little bit. "You're so good at it."

"I'm rich, handsome as fuck, and I don't give a fuck." He lifts his hands. "For some reason, women like that. At least the ones I date do. But you don't, or at least you claim to, even though you seem to keep dating men like me. So why are you here with me?"

I look away, shame burning inside me. "The last guy I dated... He said I was, and I quote, 'too uptight to fuck.'"

In my mind's eye, I can still see the curl of his lip as he said it. I remember how much it hurt. I lift a hand to my chest, feeling an echo of that same hurt.

"I just don't want that to happen again," I say quietly. "And yet I seem to keep picking the same kind of guy, each worse than the last. I want to fix it. That..." I take a deep breath. "It really hurt."

When I finally look up, Cassian is furious. Like, ready to tear something in two with his bare hands. The shift from bored playboy to... *this...* is stunning.

"I would never say that," he gets out between clenched teeth. "Not to you. Not to anyone."

Oh God. He's mad because he thinks I think he's like that. "No, I didn't mean you. Or that you're like him. It's just that you—"

"Victoria." His voice is deadly quiet. "Stop talking."

I shut my mouth, mostly out of guilt that I've hurt him.

He takes a long, slow, deep breath. "First I would never say that. No one deserves that, especially not you. You understand why he said it though?"

"Of course I do! I'm so uptight—"

Cassian blows out a sharp breath, so fast it's almost a hiss. "No, stop. Just stop." He puts one finger to his lips. "He said it because you scared him. You're so self-contained, so assured, so over any kind of bullshit—so amazing—you frightened him. And he lashed out, like cowards do."

"But I am uptight." My protest is weak because his defense of me has stolen my breath away.

"No. Not a bit. I'll show you—" He bites back whatever else he was about to say. "It's cliché, but really, it's him, not you." His voice drops to somewhere close to my buzzing nerves, playing them like harp strings. "It is *so* not you."

I swallow hard, trying to find my composure. "You see my dilemma?"

"I see you were going out with an asshole," he shoots back. "What was his name?"

I open my mouth to tell him, then catch myself. "You can't threaten a guy just because he said that to me."

"Wouldn't be a threat."

The easy lethality in that makes shivers run down my spine. Good shivers, which scares me even more.

"Just don't." I lean toward him. "Just help me avoid them. Help me find someone nice."

"*Nice.*" His lip curls. "That's definitely not me. But if that's what you want…"

It isn't. I want him, in all his wicked, twisted sensuality. But Cassian would break my heart without even meaning to. He might talk a good game about making his partner's pleasure his entire focus, but what happens when he tires of her? I'm guessing she doesn't just leave with a smile and a wave. A person doesn't just walk away from someone like Cassian.

"It is." I sit up straighter. "So you don't rehearse. How does it come so easily?"

He gives me an oddly searching look. "Let's come at this from another direction. When I'm crafting a campaign, I think of what the customer wants most. What they don't know they need. So… what do you need that you don't know about?"

His expression is so piercing I worry he can see into my soul. "I don't need anything," I say.

"There's need, and then there's *need.*"

I bet he can show me all the fine details between each of those inflections, with exquisite, glorious precision.

Maybe I need *that.*

"I don't know," I confess. "I have a good job, great friends, my family is all healthy… What more could I ask for?"

"The world. You could ask for that."

I laugh, then stop when he doesn't join in. Damn, he's serious. "Would you get me the world?"

"If you asked me."

It sounds lovely, but… "I don't need the world."

"No." He's so intensely handsome it almost hurts to look at him. "Tell me what you want. Let's start with your job. You graduated from West Point. Fricking West Point. So why aren't you still in the Army? Why are you working for someone else instead of running your own business? Why is your every thought for your friends, your family, and not for yourself?"

My throat closes so tight for a moment I struggle to breathe. My vision goes gray at the edges. I don't think I've ever been dissected so neatly. And so savagely.

"I finished out my contract," I say as best as I can. "The Army doesn't own West Pointers forever."

He snorts. "*Finished out your contract.* Everything about you still screams officer. I bet you have to stop yourself from giving Tess orders sometimes, don't you? Hell, you're at attention right now."

I suddenly realize he's right—although my pulse is pounding and my teeth are clenched, my shoulders are back, my chin up, my eyes fixed on some vague point, and my expression blank. I reached for it almost automatically.

I force myself out of it, muscle by muscle. From calm, unmoving stillness to the agitated boil I'm really feeling.

When I do, Cassian does something odd: he smiles. Not with triumph, but like he's seen something secretly amazing. "There you are, gorgeous," he says, mostly to himself.

I doubt very much that I'm gorgeous right now. I press my hands to my cheeks, feeling the angry heat there.

"Let's try this again," he says. "Why aren't you in the service any longer?"

I take a deep breath, clearing my head. "I was trained to be a leader. And to serve." At his puzzled expression, I explain, "A good leader serves the people under them. It's not about barking orders or forcing people to bend to your will. It's about taking care of them, keeping them safe. A lot of what I did was getting privates out of lockup after a crazy weekend or trying to keep them from taking out an insane car loan or just preventing what were basically teenagers from doing stupid teenaged stuff. And when we deployed…" I'm not sure how to lay that out to him, how my responsibilities to my people went from weighing an ounce to weighing a ton. "When I joined, I thought I would never leave. I thought I found my calling."

"What happened?"

"Someone higher up started harassing Tess. I went up the chain of command, did everything I was supposed to, and—" I bite my lip, hard. "Well. Anyway. I'm here and last I heard, he's up for lieutenant colonel. I guess it helps to have a dad who's a big deal at the Pentagon."

He doesn't say anything, which pushes me to say more to fill the silence he's leaving.

"They trained me to protect my people, and then when the time came, they prevented me from doing exactly that." I chip off each word like a flake of flint. "So everything I learned seemed useless after that." On the very last word, my voice breaks, careening out of my control.

Cassian reaches over and takes my hand. He's not gentle —he takes it with intent. At the touch of his skin on mine, my pulse starts to stutter. "That's not true."

I want to leave my hand in his, keep absorbing his warmth and comfort. Instead, I pull away, because I'm right and he has no idea. "They trained me to be a leader, and now I don't think I can lead anything. You want to know what I need? I need that back. And your taking me to dinner isn't going to fix that."

CHAPTER 10

As soon as Victoria opened up to me, she just as quickly shut down again.

She asked that we stop talking about it, and dinner ended soon after. But when I asked if she wanted to come over and power up the car AI, she said yes, so she can't be that angry. But she is subdued.

I open the door to my workshop, Victoria following quietly with a bowed head. Lawford isn't here, otherwise I'd ask him to make her a sandwich or bring some cake or do something to perk her up.

I pushed too hard too fast, which is something I never do. I always know the exact amount of pressure to apply—it's why I'm such a marketing genius. I've never done a hard sell.

But I did it tonight, and I scared her away. It was my own need to know more about her that drove me though, that kept me pushing even when I knew I was losing her.

The lights automatically come up when we walk in. Victoria sees all the parts arrayed around the case and sucks in a delighted breath.

"Ready to start soldering and connecting things?" I ask.

The spark in her eyes tells me she's more than ready. I guess I won't need the sandwiches after all.

I strip off my suit jacket and then start rolling up my sleeves. Victoria pauses as she reaches for one of the cables, her tongue darting out to wet her lips almost unconsciously. Her gaze is glued to my forearms. So I flex, just a touch.

Her pupils dilate.

I keep my satisfied smile to myself. Part of the reason she reacts so badly to me I suspect is that she's deeply attracted to me. And she doesn't like not being in control.

Well, I'll just have to show her how good out of control can be with me. Next lesson though—we've both had enough education for one evening.

She begins to hook up components while I test connections and make sure the thing won't catch fire once we give it some juice. Occasionally we consult the wiring diagram together, pointing out this or that. I can't help but watch her from the corner of my eye as she works.

As much as she's still completely an officer, she's also an engineer. Her fingers are eager as she pokes at parts, her movements quick and fluid. With her background, I can see even more clearly how wasted she is as Tess's employee. Not that her job is bad or that she doesn't enjoy working with her friend, but like she said, she needs more.

I'm not sure how to give her the confidence to reach for it. I can sell confidence, at least the illusion of it, but *giving* someone the real thing?

The dilemma makes me think that maybe Dad is right about me. I am just selling bullshit in the end.

"Okay," Victoria says, pulling away from the case. "I think that's it. Is everything done on your end?"

The easy command in her tone might irritate a less confident man. Luckily, she's with me and my ego is unbruisable. "Yes, ma'am."

"Good." She catches herself, blinks. "Ma'am is... It's not necessary."

"But you like it." The fact that she's perturbed proves it. "If you want, you can call me Sir. Capitalized, of course."

She turns to face me. "Are we working on this thing or are you trying to seduce me?"

"Why not both?"

Her eyes narrow. I sense danger in her expression. "I think you're trying to put off turning this thing on. You had all the parts and you didn't need my help. So why did you leave it until now?"

I don't like thinking that she might be correct. And I like having my psychoanalysis methods turned back on me even less.

"I can't help myself. That's it." I flick on the power switch to show her how wrong she is, even as cold sweat drips down my back.

The fan starts up first, whirring in a white noise rhythm that's almost as familiar as my own heartbeat. The monitor we've hooked up flashes for a moment, and then the control software for the AI pops up.

I haven't run this program in five years. Before that, it consumed my every waking thought. I saw this start-up screen every day. Seeing it now makes my heart kick in a sick way.

A pop-up screen tells me the program is communicating with the car computer. It asks what I want to do with the system now.

I release a pained breath. Some part of me, deeply buried, was hoping that it wouldn't work. That the machine would stay dark and silent, holding its secrets forever.

But that's not going to happen.

And then the fan starts to make an odd noise, like something is flapping against it. Or stuck in it.

"Shit." I flip it off quickly, the fan slowing and stopping.

"What was that?" Victoria peers inside, looking at the space between the fan and the case. "I think there's something there."

She fishes out a slip of paper, no wider than a pencil and about half as long as her finger. It looks completely ordinary at first. When she flips it over, my jaw clenches.

"That's Tynan's handwriting," I say grimly. I take it from her and try to decipher what's there.

It's a series of numbers and letters with no apparent pattern. There's about twenty-five in all, and I have no idea what it means.

"I don't understand," Victoria says.

"Neither do I." I turn the slip of paper over, looking for anything I might have missed. But there's nothing.

"Did it get in there by accident? Maybe a scrap from calculations or notes that got sealed inside?"

I shake my head. "Archer did the final check on this and sealed it up. He wouldn't have left anything behind."

"But you said Tynan probably started it up recently. Maybe it's from then?"

"It is from then. But there's no way it's an accident." I don't want to hold the slip anymore, but I don't know where to put it. It can't get lost and it's so damn small.

Fuck you, Tynan. Why couldn't you send an email like a normal person?

"It's not?" Victoria still doesn't understand, probably because she's never had to deal with her best friend thinking she tried to kill her.

"It's a message from Tynan," I say tightly. "But of course it's completely indecipherable. Asshole."

She takes it from me, and the relief I feel is immense. And unearned. This is supposed to be my problem to carry. "Maybe it's a key to the notebooks. We should give this to Archer."

Archer's the one who's working the most on decoding the notebooks, so of course she's right. "I'll do that." I take it back, slip it into my pocket where I can ignore it for a while. "If there's nothing else hiding in there, let's try again."

This time Victoria goes through it with a penlight, finding hiding places I never knew existed. "Sand can hide anywhere and everywhere," she says. "I've had to get good at hunting it down."

Finally she declares it all clear. And I start the machine up again.

This time I'm ready for the start-up screen, holding my heart rate to somewhere closer to quick rather than frantic.

"Nice user interface," Victoria says.

"Thanks. I figured it should still look good even if no one else would ever see it."

"You designed this?"

"Don't sound so surprised." I stare at the graphics for a moment, remember how I felt as I coded them. Eager, excited, unbreakable. Our car was going to conquer the auto industry and beyond. There was no way we could lose.

I don't think I've ever felt so hopeful about a project before or since. Which shows how deceptive that emotion is.

Victoria looks over the exposed chips as if she can see into the computer's function that way. "What are you going to do first?"

I take the chair in front of the keyboard, my hands hesitating over the keys. I wanted to know what really happened with this thing, but now that it's running…

Well, I'm just being a fucking coward is what. I start banging away, calling up the diagnostic subroutine. "First I want to see if everything's running and talking to everything else the way it should be. Just a simple 'How are you?' to the components."

She nods solemnly. "Right. I guess we can't just start it with simulations right away."

I'm not stalling for time, not really, but it feels that way as we work through the wiring diagram once more, checking and double-checking that each component is functional, at least on a basic level.

Before I know it, another two hours have passed. I hardly even noticed, and not only because I was engrossed in my tasks. Something about Victoria makes the time go by as if it's not happening at all.

But it's also past midnight and closing in on one in the morning.

"You doing okay?" I ask.

"Huh?" Victoria looks up from the wiring diagram. I love how lost in concentration she looks. "What do you— Oh man, it's late."

"Exactly. I can take you home and finish this up on my own. If you want." I cross my arms, although I'm not feeling as relaxed as I seem.

"No, I want to finish this." She looks back at the diagram. "Which I guess we've done."

I close out the diagnostic window. "Time for something real. Or at least real-ish." I call up a different program. "This was the very first testing program we ran on it. Let's see if it gives us the same results it did the first time."

When I hit Return and the program starts running, the hair on the back of my neck stands up. I feel like I've passed some point of no return, but I can't say why.

"How soon until we know?" She's looking surprisingly alert for having been up for hours now.

I check the progress. "Probably four to five hours."

"Hours?" Her face drops. "I really wanted to see the results."

A thought occurs to me. A dark, sinuous one.

"You could stay the night." I make my tone neutral. "We can check in the morning and you'd see as soon as it's done. Or not."

It's a lure, and I'm dangling it hard.

Here's another lesson for her: when someone wants something but is hesitant, sometimes it's best to let them fall into it all on their own.

CHAPTER 11

He's so tempting right now, and the killer part is that he knows it. He knows I want to stay, and for more than the results of the test run, and he's offering it so casually, as if to specifically drive me crazy.

If he insisted I have to stay, I'd run. Instead, he shrugs and I'm ready to fall into his arms.

But I'm going to be falling into his guest bed. "Sounds good. That way you won't have to drive so late. And I'm sure your guest bedroom is as gorgeous as the rest of this place."

His smile is wry. "Not as gorgeous as my bedroom though."

"I'll have to take your word for it."

"Will you?" he murmurs as he opens the door for me.

I don't want to—I want to see his bedroom for myself. But this is part of his routine, this smoothness. Part of the lessons he's supposed to be teaching me. If it feels all too real, that's my fault.

It could also be my confessions at dinner, things I've never told anyone but Tess. I'm on different footing here with him, more intimate, less combative. But I shouldn't mistake a cessation of fire for peace.

I close my eyes for a moment, wipe my hand over my

face. The exhaustion has suddenly hit me, the adrenaline I've been running on letting me down. My thoughts are running like a drunk hamster on a wheel.

Cassian's hand comes around my elbow. "I've got you. It's not too far." His voice is as gentle and soothing as his touch. I can feel the warmth of him along my back and side, and it's like being cocooned in comfort.

I try to recall what he said about making a person his sole entire focus as one of his tactics, but the exact details are hazy, wiped away by the sensation of him being so close. I can simply snuggle up into him and fall asleep like this.

"Here we are." He opens a door that's not too far from the workshop and reveals a room bathed in soft, golden light. The bed is literally a four-poster with gauzy fabric of slate gray hanging over it. The decor can only be described as sleek sensuality with a thick rug on the floor, an overstuffed club chair in one corner, and an honest-to-God fireplace too. It's not at all fussy, but I want to wrap myself up in it all the same.

Bruiser is sitting in one of the chairs. The expression on his furry face is tolerant, so I suppose he's accepted me as a guest. He yawns once, then pads out of the room, rubbing against Cassian's leg as he does. I guess he really does like his master.

"Nice." I cross my arms, looking over the room, trying to think of a compliment that doesn't involve praising the bed. Or how much I want to run my hands over the fabric choices, to feel the soft, slick nap under my palms. Or how good it would be to stretch out next to the fire, spreading myself out on the plush rug.

"Thanks. I chose most of it myself."

Of course he did, because he'd be amazing at that. He's so goddamn talented and attractive. I want to be mad at him. But I can't.

Cassian goes to the chest of drawers and pulls out some

tissue-wrapped packages. "Pajamas, underwear, and other clothes. These should be your size. And in the bathroom, anything else you might need."

"You just keep women's clothes on hand?" I don't mean to be accusatory, but jealousy is biting me hard.

He gives me an enigmatic smile. "I have men's clothes on hand for guests too." He hands over the packages. "If you don't like these, we can get something else."

When our fingers brush, current runs through me, scrambling my emotions even harder. We're alone with a gorgeous bed not a few feet away, and he's handing me something that's going to sit right next to my bare skin. Something that he's personally picked out, I'm sure.

The tissue comes away with the softest of sighs. And then I release a longer one of my own when I see the nightgown. It's satin, like my skirt, but heavier, lusher. The color is a deep dove gray that makes my skin glow.

It's also the exact same color of the gown I wore to Gideon's gala a week ago. I love that gown and how I looked in it.

I glance up at Cassian. "Was this deliberate?"

His smile is crooked. "I couldn't stop thinking about you in that dress. The way it clung to your curves, your skin, your eyes..." He lifts a hand as if to sketch the memory, then lets it fall. "You definitely left an impression."

I crush the nightgown to my chest, my heart hammering against my fist. This was before I offered him my help, demanded that he teach me everything he knew. This night-gown isn't part of any kind of scheme of his—it simply *is*.

"Don't look at me like that," he says roughly.

"I can't help it." I wet my lips. "You got this just for me."

He swears under his breath, crossing over to me in one quick stride. He doesn't touch me, but I feel him all over. Even the satin in my hand is hot from his nearness.

He pulls the nightgown out of my fingers, lets it drop to

the floor. "Of course I did. You came to the gala in *that* dress and didn't think every man there didn't have you seared into his eyes?"

Oh Lord, that doesn't sound like me at all. Although I did feel very wicked in that dress. "You never..."

"What was I supposed to do, fuck you right there in the middle of the best of San Francisco society?"

His anger is so real; it sizzles so hard my nipples tighten. It would have been awful to have him do that, have all those people watching us... but I can't stop imagining it.

"You wanted to do *that?*"

"To start with." He takes a half step closer so that the very tips of my breasts brush his chest. I gasp as lightning zaps through me.

"That's..." I swallow hard. "That's a lot to start with."

"Mmm." He cups my jaw. "You should stop me now if you don't want to keep going."

I turn my face, leaning into his touch. How can his hands feel so good when every other man's touch has merely been okay? "I don't want you to."

"Then let's start with this."

The first touch of our lips is short, almost sweet. A quick hello. But it still shakes me down to my toes. Cassian inhales sharply, as if he's just as affected.

The next time our mouths meet, it's deeper, longer. *I want to know you,* this kiss says. *I want to know you completely.*

I've never been kissed like this before. His lips, his tongue, the way he's holding me—it's a conversation, an interrogation, a quest.

I can't stop thinking about you in that dress.

I've imagined kissing you for so long.

I answer him back with the thrust of my tongue, the nip of my lips on his lush bottom lip, the thrust of my breasts against the hard wall of his chest. *I can't stop thinking about you. You come to my dreams, my waking fantasies.*

My pulse thickens, gathers in my core with liquid need. Even the finest movements of his lips echo through every inch of me until I'm vibrating with sustained, pitched desire.

"V," he whispers, his hot breath ghosting over my mouth, my jaw. "V."

My eyes roll back, because he was right—just that single letter is so sexy. And he's painting it on me. If he ever used that nickname in public, I might spontaneously combust. I'm dangerously close to it now.

"Cassian." I capture his wrists, needing an anchor.

"Shit," he hisses. "I think that's the first time you've ever used my name."

Is it? I can't remember. Hell, what's my name again?

"Cassian." I definitely remember his name, although I'm not certain what I'm begging him for.

He presses wild kisses along my jaw and throat. "I want you to say my name against my belly. Whisper it along my cock."

He slides a hand down my stomach as if to demonstrate. My skirt decides at that moment to ride all the way up my thighs and settle along my hips, leaving everything below my navel bare except for my panties.

His hand doesn't stop at the barrier of my skirt. Instead, he keeps traveling down and down until his fingers press a kiss against my swollen, wet folds through the fabric of my underwear.

I groan and lift my hips, pressing myself deeper into his touch. He grabs my ponytail, tilting my head back so he can devour my mouth.

And then he releases me so quickly I almost crumple. He takes one, two hard, decisive steps back. His breathing is harsh, fast, but his expression is disciplined. Although his cock, thick with need, is a sharp outline against his pants, I know he won't touch me again tonight.

With visible effort, he brings his breathing under control.

Such mastery is impressive to see. He reaches out and, very carefully not touching my skin, tugs my skirt into place.

"Get some sleep." His tone is half affection, half gruffness. "I'll come get you when the testing is complete."

I wrap my arms around myself, needing something now that he's so far away. "Won't you sleep?"

He laughs grimly as he heads for the door. "After that? No way." He pauses in the doorframe, his gaze so hot my lungs start to sear. "Honestly, I haven't had a decent night's sleep since I met you."

And then he leaves me to wrestle with that.

CHAPTER 12

The program finally finishes right as the sun is coming up.

I take a sip of my espresso and scroll through the results. My office is quiet, even with both the cats in here. Bane is actually almost sitting at my feet—five feet away counts as close for him. Bruiser's doing his best to take over my entire desk.

I push the massive cat aside so I can actually reach my keyboard. I know I said I'd wake Victoria up as soon as it was done, but she needs the rest. And I want to look first, in case there's any nasty surprises.

She already knows I'm probably responsible for someone's death with this thing, but if the test shows that something I designed personally failed...

After last night, I don't want to see that disappointment in her eyes.

I read through lines and lines of results, some of it only decipherable to me and the rest of the guys. I blow out a long breath when I reach the end.

Nothing. The AI passed every initial test with flying colors. If there's something wrong, it's deeper than this simple pass can find.

I push the keyboard away. This is what I thought might

happen, but I'm still annoyed. I just want to know what the fuck happened, and I want to know now. Tynan's little games aren't funny.

I reach into my pocket, pull out the slip of paper Victoria found inside the case. The numbers and letters don't make any more sense than they did last night.

"Motherfucker," I mutter. "You couldn't just appear and explain everything. Had to turn it into a game."

Unless he's luring us into some trap to exact his revenge. If he thinks we tried to kill him on purpose, it's very possible.

I'd almost rather that be true—at least then the irritation I'm feeling would be more justified. I can be mad at a guy trying to kill me even if I did almost kill him.

With one last curse, I put the paper back into my pocket. Picking up my phone, I call Lawford.

"Sir?" Even at six in the morning, he sounds totally unflappable.

"Victoria very much likes your sandwiches. Do you think you could put together a breakfast version?"

"She spent the night then."

"In the guest room." And I spent the night in this work-shop, pacing the floor, because I couldn't sleep with her so close.

Patience sucks so hard sometimes.

"Very good," Lawford says with utmost blandness. "Should I take it to her, or would you prefer to do it?"

"I should do it. I promised to show her something this morning, and she'll be mad if I don't follow through."

"We don't want that."

Indeed we didn't. Fifteen minutes later I'm carrying a tray with a pretty impressive breakfast sandwich on it into the guest bedroom.

Victoria's eyes snap open the moment the door swings open. Not a light sleeper then.

When she sees me, her lips part and a hunger comes into

her eyes. I'd almost guess I woke her up from a dream about me. Her gaze runs over me, lingering at all the places I'm aching for her.

"I warned you about looking at me like that." I walk toward her, tempted to toss the breakfast tray aside. She deserves to lose her breakfast after mentally undressing me like that.

"Is the test finished running?" she asks, taking the tray from me. She inhales appreciatively. "I thought you said Lawford only knows how to make sandwiches."

"You don't think I made this?" I drag the chair closer to the bed and sprawl in it.

She rolls her eyes. "You have a butler. Why would you ever cook?"

It's a fair point. "So how does Lawford's breakfast sandwich compare with the other one?"

"I'll let you know." She takes in the tray with the sandwich, coffee, fruit, and the single rosebud in a tiny vase. "I've never had breakfast in bed before."

My eyebrows shoot up. "Not ever?"

She shakes her head. "It feels decadent to start eating before I've even gotten out of bed."

"What, you should immediately hop out and start doing jumping jacks?"

Her cheeks color. "Well, I do have a morning routine."

Oh how intriguing. I gesture to the open space in the middle of the room. "Please. Go ahead."

"I'm not doing it in front of you," she mutters.

"Pretend I'm not here."

"As if." She takes a sip of coffee, sighs appreciatively. "What did the results say?"

I give her a wounded look, mostly because she's not going to do some yoga for me. "I told you I'd let you know the moment it finished. I wouldn't have time to look."

"You looked." She sets down her cup. "What did it say?"

"Nothing." I give a half shrug. "All systems normal, everything reacting as it should. It can see the road, identify features, react to obstacles, respond to road signs... everything it should be doing according to the vehicle code."

"No one drives according to the vehicle code."

I can't help my smile. "Been thinking a lot about four-way stops lately?"

"You said it yourself: the hardest part is predicting human behavior. Since you designed that part, I assume you have a test for it."

I feel a pulse of pride that she noticed that my problem was the most difficult to solve. "I do. Morgan sent over a couple of the test sets they use on the Inspiron operating system. It's more advanced than any of the sets we used before."

The price for those is allowing Morgan to test the system on her own. Once I'm done putting it through its paces and trying to get it to break down, I have to hand it over to her.

She's going to be ruthless, which is what we need. But I'm also frightened of what she'll find. If there's a fatal error in the system, I want to root it out first. It's our mistake and we need to own it.

"Then let's start running those." Victoria sets aside the tray and throws off the covers.

Immediately every inch of me goes hard.

She's wearing the nightgown, which is pushed up to midthigh, revealing her long, well-defined legs. This woman hasn't skimped on the PT since she left the Army. I saw her legs last night, but like this, with the nightgown revealing more than it conceals and the fabric highlighting every curve I want to trace with my hands and mouth, it sets me off.

I throw the blanket aside, sending the breakfast tray to the floor with a wild clatter. Her eyes go wide, her breath coming fast. I climb up her until we're nose to nose, her thighs between mine. I take a fistful of the nightgown, heavy and slick in my palm.

"If I'd known how this nightgown was going to look on you..." I tug it up another inch.

"What?" She's so breathless my cock twitches. "You wouldn't have bought it?"

"Wrong." I brush my mouth along the edge of her jaw, the skin so soft there I want to never lift my head. "I would have bought more. All of them. The entire factory, just making these nightgowns for you."

She lifts up into me, her center pressing against my growing erection. As she does, her nightgown settles around her waist, held in place by my hand. I grind my hips into the place I want to be, kept apart by a few flimsy layers of fabric.

"I don't know if I want you to tear it or not," Victoria says, her eyes closed.

I should tear it. She needs more chaos, needs to release some of that control and let her wildness free.

But I hold back. Tearing it would be putting my needs first, and I'm making her the focus, not me. She needs to be coaxed into letting go of all that control wrapping her into knots, not pushed into it.

I release the nightgown. Time for some coaxing. I lift up onto one arm, setting my other hand into her rib cage. God, how can a rib cage be that perfect? But it is, the curves of her meeting my grip as if I were made especially for her.

"Victoria." I wait until she opens her eyes. "Watch me."

The shocked heat that flares in her gaze is so gratifying. I run my hand up her torso until I reach the underside of her breast. Another perfect curve, just waiting for me to fit myself to it.

So I do. Her mouth opens wide on a silent gasp.

"Feels good, doesn't it?" I slide the satin over her skin, over her tight nipple. "Not even skin on skin and it already feels so good."

Her mouth stays closed, and somehow that makes my teeth grind together.

"Tell me," I say. "Tell me how it feels." She doesn't get to be so closed off, not with me. I'm the one she opens up to. She owes me at least that much.

"I want your bare hand." It's not what I ordered her to say—it's even better.

"Maybe," I allow, even though I want it too. "But I like teasing you like this." I pluck at her nipple as I roll my hips into the cradle of her pelvis.

"Is this part of your plan?" She's panting.

"No, this is spontaneous." I nip at her collarbone, savor her gasp. "But here's another lesson: never make it easy. And never miss an opportunity to make it hard."

She busts out a reluctant laugh. "That's a terrible joke. Just awful."

"But you still laughed." Something about her laughter as we're hot and frantic against each other unwinds something in me—and winds up even tighter something else.

"I couldn't help it." Her voice is soft with realization. Like she's stopped to consider exactly where we are and she... she likes it.

I run my fingers along the inside of her thigh, the skin like superheated silk. "Good. I want you to love it so much you can't help anything. Even laughing."

Her thighs fall apart another inch, and I fall deeper into the center of her. It would be the work of a moment to be inside her. But it's too soon. And that would be too selfish of me. I haven't even given her an orgasm yet.

So I slide down her body, her nightgown clinging to me as much as it is to her. My hands find her knees, hold her open for me. Already the scent of her arousal is in the air.

Goddamn the man who told her she was too uptight. She's so responsive it makes my head spin. If you crash a race car because you're a shitty driver, you shouldn't blame the car. Although comparing her to a car feels weak, inadequate. Like her ex-boyfriends.

I'm going to obliterate the memory of those men for her right now. I run my fingers over the damp fabric covering her folds, using her panties to heighten the sensation of what I'm doing. Her clit is so swollen and needy it's like a beacon to my touch.

Victoria moans and thrashes, fighting the rising tide of pleasure. I don't tell her to stop, to give in, because she needs this, needs to kick and shove as it takes over, needs that last battle before giving in to the ultimate surrender.

And her surrender is going to be so good.

I stroke her clit, picking up the pace as her struggles increase. Her hips lift and she bucks, but I'm not going anywhere. We're riding this out together.

"You can't help it," I say harshly. "It's so good you can't fight it."

She bares her teeth at me, and I've never seen anything more erotic. My erection is painfully hard as it presses into her thigh, but I ignore it.

So close. I sense the tide in her rising, ready to pull her under. I stroke faster, hooking my middle finger under her panties to trace her folds, then find her heated center. Holy fuck, but she feels amazing around me, hot and soft and wet as my dreams of her.

When she comes, she melts. There's no other way to describe it. One moment she's rolling like she might still escape that orgasm, and the next... Everything stills and she sinks into herself, going soft and sensual as the silk of her nightgown.

I'm torn between triumph and awe. Triumph because I was right about her becoming all softness when she gave in. Awe because she's so fucking glorious when she does, even beyond my wildest imaginings.

I push myself up until we're face-to-face, the better to

watch her expression. It's dreamy and content, a half smile on her lips. I want to taste that smile so badly my mouth tingles. My heart also does a weird kick flip as her eyes open.

"Mmmm." The noise she makes matches her expression perfectly. "That was—"

Her phone rings. I bite back some nasty words about whoever the fuck would dare to call right now.

"Ignore it," I command. "Finish what you were saying."

"It's Tess." She pushes weakly against my chest. "She's worried about me."

"Jesus." I roll off and toss my arm over my eyes. "Are you two attached at the hip?" I lift my arm. "If Gideon starts talking shit, tell him I said to fuck off."

"I will not." She searches through her purse, coming up with her phone. "Hello?" she says into the speaker. "No, I'm fine. Seriously, everything is okay."

I get up, adjusting myself when I stand. I can't do anything about my erection at the moment, but at least I can smooth out the rest of me. *Always be in control of your own need.* That would be a lesson I could teach her, except I'm not good proof of it at the moment. She's managed to spin me out of my orbit and trap me in hers.

That thought should worry me. Funny that it doesn't.

Before I can ponder it further, she tosses down the phone. The nightgown slithers over her curves as she turns to me. "Okay, let's go see it."

"There's nothing interesting in the results," I say. "We'd have more fun back in bed."

For a moment her discipline breaks and she glances at the bed. She's tempted. Massively tempted. With a deep inhale, she pulls her armor back into place. "No. I want to see the data."

But she also wants to be back in bed with me. Holding in my smile of triumph, I head for the door.

"Wait for me," she says, eyes widening.

"I will. Outside."

Her brow creases in puzzlement.

I let my gaze run over her as thoroughly as I'd like my hands to. "You might want to change before you come out."

Her breathing slows and deepens as if I really was caressing her. "Yeah," she says distantly. "I should change."

When I shut the door behind me, I finally let my smile out. Teaching her how to handle a man like me is turning out to be way more satisfying than I ever dreamed.

Cassian was right. There was nothing interesting in the preliminary results.

It's Monday, and I'm back at work but on my lunch break, looking through the data from the tests we ran this weekend. Cassian let me take a copy of the results, so I spent all day yesterday digging through it, searching for something to prove him wrong. But there's nothing so far.

"You should do something mindless," Tess chides me from her desk. "Staring at a screen all day will make you go blind."

"I went for a run this morning," I say without looking up. "And I'll hit the gym tonight."

At least that was my plan this morning. But I'm tempted to skip the gym to keep going through this data.

"Work and working out don't count as mindless," Tess says. "You need downtime too."

I sigh and push the laptop away because she's right. If I burn out, I won't have the mental stamina to go through the results Cassian is generating with the data sets Morgan gave him. That's the important stuff.

Or you could do a field test.

I don't know where the idea came from, but it makes me sit up straighter. "They haven't run it in a car yet."

Tess blinks. "Are you talking about the self-driving program?"

Crap, she doesn't know what I've been immersed in the past two days. She does know that the date with Cassian went... okay. I told her about my outburst at dinner, and she was understanding. She also didn't tell me it was a good thing that I lost my cool with him since she knows what I'm like. Losing control is always bad for me.

I mentioned that I slept in his guest room but *not* that he gave me an amazing orgasm the next morning. Tess said Cassian was being quite the gentleman, and I was too overcome with the memories of how wicked he can be to contradict her.

"Yes, the car computer." I gesture to my laptop. "We ran some initial tests and everything looks fine. But what if we just cut to the chase and try to reproduce the conditions that made it fail the first time?"

"*Fail?* It killed two people. And you want to put it back into a car?"

"We'll be ready for it to fail this time," I say. "It's just... I feel like we're wasting time with feeding it fake scenarios. They did that before and thought it was fine. To get it to be not fine, you have to put it back where it failed before."

Tess's expression clouds. "I already know where you're going with this, and no. I'm telling you no."

I set my jaw. "I never said what I was going to do."

"You don't have to. If you're going to suggest something like this, of course you're going to offer to do it yourself. You'd never put someone else in danger. You'd take point, the way you always do."

Okay, maybe she does know me way too well, because that's what I was thinking. "I wouldn't drive it near a cliff," I say stiffly. "It'd be in a parking lot."

"How is that not also artificial?" Tess points out. "There's no one else driving in an empty lot. And you could still die.

What if the car flips? Or accelerates into a wall or something?"

Something tickles the back of my mind, something about the empty lot… And then it becomes so clear I'm furious I didn't see it sooner.

"Cassian is the people person," I say to Tess, as if that makes perfect sense. "That's why Tynan sent it to him."

"Cassian is a player," Tess says, correcting me. "And what does that have to do with driving?"

I gesture in front of me as if to clear out the cobwebs. "No, no. The thing is, all driving is reacting to others. Reading the tiny details in how a car moves to read the driver's mind. It's as much understanding subtle social cues as it is simply steering the car. Actually maybe more. And that's what Cassian was in charge of. Programming in the human element."

Tess is beginning to get it. "So you think that's where it failed? Which is why Cassian got the box sent to him?"

I lift my palms. "It makes the most sense. So therefore, we've got to get out there with real people, try to react to them."

"That's way more dangerous than taking it out in an empty lot," Tess says solemnly.

"I know," I say just as solemnly. "But I think that's what we have to do."

"Not you." Tess raises her index finger. "This is their problem, and there's no way Gideon would let you be in the car to test it."

"Cassian wouldn't either," I say without thinking.

Tess raises an eyebrow. "Interesting."

"Look," I sputter. "He's not a monster. It's not like he's going to use me as a test dummy."

No, he has very different plans for my body. Much more interesting plans. There's no way I would admit it to him, but I was pretty annoyed with Tess for calling right when she did. I know she was worried, but she could have waited an hour. Or maybe even longer.

"Oh, I know he wouldn't," Tess says. "But the way you said that… as if he has a deeper, more intimate reason to forbid you. You were all alone in that guest room of his? All night long?"

"He wasn't there at night," I say weakly. "He might have come in with breakfast in bed for me though."

Tess's mouth drops open. "Cassian brought you breakfast in bed and you hadn't even slept with him? That's…" Her eyes narrow. "*Romantic.*"

"I'm only using him, I swear." My voice teeters dangerously. "It's not anything more than that. He just knows I really like sandwiches."

"He made you a breakfast sandwich?"

I nod, not trusting my voice.

"Oh." Tess puts her hands to her cheeks. "Oh. You really like those."

The worry in her face has my back going rigid. "He's not going to entrap me with meat stuffed between bread products."

"What happened after he brought you breakfast?"

Oh Lord. "We, uh… we messed around. But that was part of our deal."

"The sandwiches weren't. Him worrying about you wasn't."

My shoulders sink. "So what's your point?"

Tess bites her lower lip. "I don't know. I don't think he's heartless or that he'd intentionally hurt you. And I know you think that having this deal between you means you're going in with your eyes wide open… but things happen. And they happen so fast you never see them coming." She smiles wryly. "Take it from me. It worked out perfectly in my case, but…" She shrugs helplessly. "These guys are potent. I mean,

Gideon is the most potent of all, but Cassian is pretty serious too."

Cassian is way more potent than Gideon, but I'm too loyal to say that to Tess. "I'll be careful. It was a good sandwich, but not that good."

Now the orgasm… that might be a different story.

"You also can't test the car computer," Tess says. "As your friend, I'm putting my foot down and saving you from yourself. But I think you might be right about testing it in more real-world situations. I never figured Cassian as the one to model the human responses though."

I bristle before I remember I used to think that too. "He actually is really good at reading people. It's deeper than that—he's really good at understanding behavior."

"I guess you'd have to be if you want to sell things to people."

I shake my head. "But it's more than that. If anything, marketing is smaller than his talent. He's genuinely fascinated by human behavior."

"Huh." Tess tilts her head. "He definitely doesn't give off that vibe."

No, he wouldn't, because it would make him seem vulnerable. His attitude is his own kind of armor. I wonder what he's protecting himself from.

"Trust me, he's deeper than he appears." I reach for my phone. "And I should tell him that we need to put that computer in a car immediately."

"But not with you." Tess's tone is firm.

"Sure," I say, although I might be bending the truth a bit. It feels wrong to let someone else take on the danger. Tess is right though—this isn't my mission. I'm only helping out in an ancillary way.

When Cassian answers, I don't even bother with hello. "Stop running Morgan's data sets. I've figured it out."

CHAPTER 14

Archer is looking at the scrap of paper we found inside the case, his brow tight as he reads off the numbers and letters again and again. He flips it over, flips it back, his expression never loosening.

So he can't make sense of it either. I lean back against my chair with a muttered "Fuck." I knew it was a long shot, but I still hoped.

"Inside the case," Archer says, mostly to himself. "But Tynan couldn't have known about the notebooks." He reaches for his laptop, starts typing. "Still, it's something to go on."

"Decoding isn't going so well, huh?"

I look around Archer's office, which isn't as professor-ish as one might expect. Yeah, he does machine translations for a living, but it's not like he reads for fun. Which makes his career path all the weirder. Why try to get a computer to translate poems you can't understand even in English?

The media doesn't care that he doesn't read much in real life though, because I've crafted branding for him that makes them not care. *Language is no longer a barrier.* It's a tagline that every reporter repeats about him, because my media team has planted it in their subconscious with every story about

Archer. He's tearing down barriers, making stories and literature available to everyone in the world. And I even have them mention something about saving dying languages with his translation software.

He's been one of my best branding projects. People completely buy the hype about him. Not that it's all hype—he really is building the best machine translation software, and he has helped document several dying languages. But I've taken what's real and made it better.

"I've digitized all the notebooks," Archer says, still typing rapidly. "I'm running it through a linguistics program, trying to see if there're any patterns like grammar it can pick up. Maybe if I can see patterns of speech, I can start decoding it with that approach."

"But you haven't yet."

He stops typing, stares straight at me. "No. What else is happening with the self-driving computer?"

"It's running." I shrug. "As far I can tell, no major problems. It passed the initial tests, and it's passing through Morgan's data sets without any errors. If something is wrong, it's deep in there."

"So deep we couldn't ever see it?"

"That won't absolve us." My mouth twists and I force it to straighten. "A mistake we couldn't see is still a mistake, especially if it was a fatal one."

"I wasn't looking for absolution." Archer goes back to typing, never saying what he was looking for. "Ah. There's something interesting."

"What?" A sharpness runs down my spine, although I keep my posture relaxed. And I don't get up to see.

Archer turns the screen to me. "Over four hundred hits in the notebooks for this. Definitely not random."

Son of a bitch. I work my jaw, trying to puzzle it all out. "Are we sure Tynan didn't know about the journals?"

"Of course not," Archer says. "We're not sure about

anything when it comes to him. But if we take the simplest explanation—he didn't know—this relates to something Ira was working on that Tynan did know about. And maybe we knew too; we just don't know how it relates to the project."

"Ira was working on the neuronal-interface stuff. I mean, that's what he was always working on, from the beginning." It's no secret what Ira's work was—it made him rich and famous. Getting computers to talk to our nervous system has been a science fiction dream for so long, but Ira was making it happen.

Archer rubs his chin. "Have you shown this to Oscar?"

I stare at him. "Of course not. Oscar has no idea what we did."

"Unless Morgan or Raven told him."

I remember my last call with Oscar, where he was so warm, so supportive. Like my dad never is. Like Oscar always is. "There's no way they told him. But look, how do we know Tynan didn't know about the notebooks before Ira died? He sent someone to steal his."

That's what started this entire mess off—an unknown intruder breaking into Gideon's fortress and trying to take Tynan's notebook.

Archer steeples his fingers. "The will was public record. Tynan could have found out about them there. If we assume Tynan did know about the notebooks before we did, then we'll never get anywhere with decoding this. But if he didn't and it relates to something we know Ira was working on, then it gives us a foothold."

Sometimes Archer is so relentlessly logical it freaks me out. "You think too much."

"Someone around here has to." He pulls the laptop back. "Have you googled the string?"

"Of course. The only thing of interest that came back was a chip serial number, but it was the kind of thing you'd buy at Fry's to make Baby's First Logic Gate."

Archer frowns at his laptop screen. "You're right."

"Did you really think Tynan was going to leave us a clue that we could just google?" I point to the laptop. "Get into Ira's archives. Let's search those."

Archer starts to connect to them. "You know, we don't really know Tynan anymore. We can't assume he'll behave like he did before."

"I wasn't." It's been weighing on my mind, this notion that Tynan is a complete mystery to us now. We were closer than brothers, and now he's a shadow sending us sinister clues that make no sense.

The old Tynan wasn't exactly an open book, but he wouldn't have done something like this. But that's the point —we're not dealing with the old Tynan.

Which means I can't predict what he'll do next.

Archer glances over at me. "What's wrong?"

I smooth out my expression. "Nothing."

"You had a weird look. Like you were upset. Except you never look upset."

Damn right. I let myself slip up there. "I said it's nothing. Your search is done."

That drags Archer's attention right back to his laptop. "Huh. This is weird." He types as he frowns at the screen. "What is this?"

I resist the urge to lean over him to see. "I don't know. You tell me."

Archer sucks in a deep breath, lets it out slowly, completely. "There's a directory that has our mystery string as its name. But it's password protected, and I suspect it's encrypted too. It says it was created four months before Ira died."

I sit up. "Ira wrote his will four months before he died." I only remember that because the date the will was drafted was Gage's unbirthday. Raven threw a party for him, and it was the last time we were all together, Ira, Oscar, the girls, and us guys. Raven started this thing where we celebrated unbirthdays, the date six months after your real birthday. She kept it up even after Ira died.

I wonder if she'll keep doing it now that she knows we were responsible for the crash. Bishop's unbirthday is coming up in a week—I guess we'll find out.

"He hasn't labeled any other directory like this," Archer says as he scrolls with the mouse. "They're all named something descriptive. Except for this."

"What's the main directory it's in?"

Archer shakes his head. "None. It's just sitting there on its own, not part of any other substructure."

"So we've got to crack it open if we want to know what's in it."

Archer rubs a hand over his face. "We were always going to have to do that. I'll hand it off to Gage. Christ, this thing just keeps getting more tangled."

I knock my fist against the desk as I think. If Ira set up this folder four months before he died and put together the notebooks and finalized his will… "What were we doing with the AI four months before the crash?"

"Golf cart testing," Archer immediately answers. "Last test on the golf cart was two weeks before Gage's unbirthday. We installed it in the first car three days after the party."

"And we put it in Ira's car two weeks before the crash." Which was way too soon, in hindsight.

"We had tens of thousands of hours of testing on the first car," Archer says as if he can read my mind. "We thought it was solid."

It's true—there wasn't a moment where one of us wasn't driving the test car, pushing the self-driving system to its limits. Hell, Bishop even took it off-roading, sending it skidding around curves like a rally car. And with no errors at all.

"We were cocky," I say.

"I know." That carries more weight than two simple words should.

I think some more, trying to come at the problem from a new angle. Or problems, plural. They're piling up now.

"What if we tell Oscar about the files?" I ask. "If it was related to whatever they were working on, he might know the password. Or be able to guess at it."

Archer raises an eyebrow. "And how do we explain how we came across it? It's just some random directory in the archives."

I shrug. "The archives are massive. We say we were looking for something else, came across this weird file, and thought it might be important. He opens it for us, probably shows us what it is because he's just that nice, and our problem is solved."

"Is it?" Archer asks quietly. "Haven't we lied enough to Oscar?"

We have. But this isn't a lie. "Look, if it was something they were working on, it belongs to him anyway. Or at least partly to him. And we were looking for something else, technically."

"Do you ever wonder why Oscar never did anything more with the neuronal-interface projects after Ira died?"

"Of course I did. But it's obvious—he'd lost his best friend and partner and he was already rich enough." Even as I say it, I realize it's wrong. Oscar's nice, but he's not a pushover. Before Ira died, I would have said he was even more driven than Ira.

"Are we really doing all this because we want to be rich enough?"

I shake my head. "No, but that's us. We do this because we're driven to know, to build, to create things at the frontiers of tech. Oscar might have been like that once, but he changed after Ira died. We all did."

I'm thinking most particularly of Tynan and the black hole he's turned into.

Archer stares at the computer screen for a long moment. "I guess you're right," he finally says. "I'll let you tell Oscar about it. You're better at... that kind of stuff." He means lying, fast-talking, scamming. And he's not wrong.

"I'm also closest to Oscar."

"Of course. That's what I meant too."

I have no intention of telling him that he definitely didn't, and my phone rings before I could even if I wanted to.

When I see that it's Victoria calling, I can't help my smile. I can't pretend not to be affected by her reaching out.

"Hey." My tone is husky, warm. Archer's attention pricks up.

"Stop running Morgan's data sets. I've figured it out."

"Absolutely not." I shake my head as I pace my workroom. "There's no way we're ever putting that back into a car."

Victoria merely watches me, her expression set. "If you want to reproduce the error…"

She makes it sound like I don't. Which of course I do. "We could put it on another golf cart. Or a parking lot."

Now she shakes her head like she's had this argument with me before. "Something deeper is going on here. Otherwise, why is Tynan doing all this? He wants you to repeat the scenario that led to the accident but can't do it himself for whatever reason."

I stop dead and stare at her. "How do you figure that?" She's never met Tynan, has no idea what he's like. It makes a kind of sense, at least as much sense as anything in this does.

Except I know she's going to insist on being in the car. And just the thought leaves me so cold I could shatter.

She shrugs. "I was trying to look for what Tynan might be trying to achieve with all this. I mean, beyond revenge, although this is way too convoluted for that. He wants his notebook because it's his property and he thinks there're clues in there. So he takes it, but in secret. And he sends you the self-driving system because he can't figure out the error on his own."

"He sends it to me because I fucked up," I say bitterly. "Something about the predictions for other drivers' behavior is off. And it almost killed him."

"Maybe," she allows. "I definitely think he sent it to you for a particular reason. The human behavior part of the system could be faulty somewhere. Or..." She holds her breath.

"Or...?" I prompt impatiently.

"Or someone close to you betrayed you. And he needs you to use your people-reading skills to root them out."

I sit down heavily. I knew it was a possibility, and certainly Gideon suspected all of us when the first break-in occurred. But...

What if I can't? The question bounces around my skull, activating all my deepest fears. Maybe my dad is right—I'm only a scammer, good for selling people shit they don't need. Certainly that's what Victoria thinks about me.

Rooting out an evil right in the very middle of the people closest to me? A scammer could never do that.

I set my hands on the workbench, palms down. Victoria's been so quiet, as if she knows what I'm wrestling with.

"Who then?" I ask. Not that she can answer. And maybe even I won't be able to in the end.

She shifts, swallows hard. "Well, there're the other guys. Gideon seems to think it wasn't any of you, but what if he's wrong?"

I go through each of them in turn. Gideon... if it is him, he's gone to some crazy lengths to throw suspicion off himself. Gideon isn't that devious in the end.

"Not Gideon," I say. "This isn't him at all. He might be a bastard, but he comes straight at a thing. Usually."

Victoria visibly relaxes. I suppose she wouldn't want her

best friend's boyfriend to be guilty of something like that. "Gage?"

Gage. The security guy. Not a talker. He knows how to keep things buried. But the truth is, if he wanted Tynan dead, he'd be dead. Gage doesn't leave loose ends. And while he's gotten more skilled as he's come up in the world, he was still damn effective when he was young.

But why would he betray Ira? Or any of us?

The question has been tearing at me. Ira loved us, nurtured us. Losing him… He was irreplaceable.

Yeah, we all got a nice inheritance out of his will, but it wasn't like he was stingy with us. He owed us nothing and gave us everything.

If someone only wanted the money…

"I'm the most likely suspect," I say woodenly. "The profile fits me. And pretty much only me."

Maybe that was Tynan's message: *I know you did it. Here's your murder weapon back.*

"I don't understand." Victoria's tone is gentle, but she's clearly confused.

Because she doesn't know me. Not at all.

"Do you know the story of how Ira found me?" My voice is quiet in the loud silence between us.

"No. I understand that you all were… troubled."

"*They* were troubled. I was a criminal."

I say it casually, carelessly, as if there isn't a sharp ache behind my chest. My crimes were all committed as a juvenile, so no reporter has ever uncovered them. I also paid a lot to have them buried and never spoken of. Maybe my empire wouldn't have suffered if my past became widely known. Maybe it would have added to the devil-may-care air I cultivated.

I didn't want to find out though, so I made sure no one else could find out.

"You were a kid," Victoria says. "There's nothing on you as an adult."

I smile in spite of myself. "Of course you looked."

Her cheeks go pink. "I work in security. I look at everyone's record."

"No, it's smart," I say. "Which reminds me, I owe you more lessons."

But maybe she won't want those anymore, not when she learns the full extent of what I did. Not my little upright soldier girl.

"You do," she says simply. "But I want to finish what you were telling me."

A weight I didn't even know was there lifts from my chest. "I was a scammer. I started with email scams and moved up from there."

Her nose wrinkles. "Like those awfully written emails that ask for five hundred dollars so you can eventually send them their inheritance or something? Because of crazy banking rules?"

I rear back. "What? No, my emails were good. You've seen my Instagram; do you think I could ever write something so sloppy?"

"I haven't seen your Instagram." She sniffs. "So what were the emails like?"

I try to recall one of my better ones. "There was one… I'm trying to remember it. I never asked for an insane amount. Not at first."

When I started out, I was only thinking about making some extra grocery money. A fifty I could slip to my mom so she wouldn't have to agonize over buying the cheapest cuts of meat, the almost-expired breads. By the time I got good at it—and we were in deeper financial straits—I asked for more. And got it.

Victoria raises her brows. "Insane amounts?"

"Well, they seemed insane at the time." I put on a crooked

smile. "Now it's what I'd spend on a slow Saturday night. But at the time…" Suddenly it comes to me. "So, the most successful asks were when I'd tell a story. I spun this story about a charity run entirely by kids. I made up the email address, the website, and even set up a bank account."

It was so much work as I piled on detail after detail in the scheme, building the perfect story about this charity. Even though it was all lies, I was so proud of it. It was my first branding attempt.

"You set up a bank account as a kid?" Victoria's tone drips disbelief.

I shrug. "You can do anything on the internet. It was a charity for homeless pets. Kids helping pets, and I asked for ten dollars to buy a bag of dog food. Or cat food. The website had some pretty touching pictures."

She's gone rigid now, as if I told her I stole straight from a cancer patient's wallet.

"I never stole from anyone," I say. "They all gave me the money freely."

"Because you lied to them." She's so implacable. "Lies about kids and animals. Animals you never intended to help."

She makes it sound as if I spend my days kicking puppies down the street. I actually set up a foundation that funds the entire humane society of San Francisco, but I'm not about to tell her that. Her judgment reminds me too much of my dad's.

"Yeah, well, they gave me the money and we were able to get groceries that week." My tone is too bitter, but I can't seem to stop. "And after that, when I got better at selling lies, I got enough to pay the mortgage. So we got to keep our house. And pay the medical bills. When I told my dad how I got the money, he wore the exact same expression you are now. But he still took it when I offered."

She simply watches me for a long moment. "So you did it for your family."

I shake my head—I don't want her letting me off that easy. "No, I did it for me. To prove I could. The money helped, but mostly I did it to throw it in my dad's face."

Her eyes narrow. "What about your mom? Where was she?"

I look away because I don't want to talk about this. It's not that it hurts—it's more like rubbing at the memory of a wound than the real thing. But I still don't want to.

Not that Victoria would let me get away with that.

"She was busy with other things. She had hepatitis C."

God, I hate that word, that whole string of syllables. It's the ugliest thing I've ever forced out of my mouth.

Victoria is quiet, a sponge for my bitter mood. She takes it up solemnly, as if it's her duty. But a good one. "I'm so sorry."

Of course she already knows. Anyone who's delved into my background knows my mom isn't around anymore. But not the hows and whys.

"She was sick for a long time." I find myself speaking without even consciously deciding to. "And we weren't rolling in money even before that. He hated how I got the money, but like I said, my dad still took it. He was that desperate. Mom… she never knew the full extent of what I'd done. She died before I got arrested."

"Which was where Ira found you."

Anyone else would dwell on what happened to Mom— the details, how long she was sick, how I felt about it. But Victoria pushes me to the next part. The part I originally meant to tell her. Funny how she got more out of me than I ever intended without really trying.

I nod. "Finally they caught me. I was sentenced to about ten years since I was an adult when they arrested me and forbidden from touching a computer for the rest of my life."

She frowns. "Can they do that?"

"They can do anything they want. One day, while I was

waiting to be transferred to the prison where I'd serve out my term, Ira appeared with a lawyer in tow. He'd heard about my exploits and thought my talents could be put to better use under his supervision. He got me out and on the path to something on the right side of the law."

"You guys talk about him as if he's this kind, fatherly type of guy," she says. "But he clearly had a lot of power."

I shrug. "He was both things. Many things, actually. A genius, a driven businessman, a kind but distant father to his girls, a foster father to us. And one of the other guys may describe him entirely differently."

She puts her chin in her hand. "Based on what Tess has said, I don't think Gideon sees the distant father."

No, he wouldn't. Gideon can be very black-and-white—Ira was a better father to him than his own, so of course Ira would be a good father to his own girls.

"It's true," I say. "Raven… she always sees the bright side, so I don't think Ira's parenting hurt her as much, but Morgan's definitely aware of it."

"Aware enough to try to hurt him?" She raises an eyebrow. "Because no matter what you say about being the suspect, I know it wasn't you."

"What makes you so sure?" I challenge her. "I just told you I ended up in jail. I scammed people out of thousands of dollars. For all their screwups, none of the other guys ever ended up as a criminal."

"Because once Ira saved you, you stayed saved," she says simply. "Why hurt him when he was the only one who believed in you?"

I catch a sharp inhale. "What makes you think I'm capable of that kind of loyalty? I'm the bad boy, the one to avoid. The one who'll only break your heart."

Something like surprise flares in her eyes. Like she's just now remembering that she's supposed to be wary of me.

"You're not really going to break my heart," she says uncertainly. "It was only a deal, nothing more."

"Was it?" I ask silkily. This is familiar ground, me encouraging her to more, to what she really needs. "What was that orgasm I gave this morning then? Only tit for tat?"

She puts her hand to her throat, her pulse fluttering under her skin. God, but she gets so flustered when I turn her on. So fucking charming and innocent. "It was... a lesson?"

I lean in, the better to see how her eyes darken. "Was it? I think you might need another one."

She licks her lips, and I only just hold back from kissing her. "I'm not going to forget what you told me. You can't distract me."

"I bet I can have you forgetting your own name." My pulse is loud in my ears, and I wonder if I might forget my name too if I let this spin out like it's threatening to.

"Probably," she allows. "But not that."

The way she says it, like my story is branded on her heart now... I give in then and capture her mouth, her waist, and pull all of her up out of her chair and into my body.

CHAPTER 16

He's right—I probably will forget my own name. His mouth is so demanding, so greedy, there's no room inside me for anything but my own need.

Maybe I've already forgotten it. Certainly my brain can't summon anything but *want* and *hurry* and *now*. This kiss is unlike any other he's given me; abandoned, wild, spinning off its axis into crazy new dimensions.

Usually he's been controlled, pushing me to my limits, then past them. This time he's the one past his limits.

"V." He groans that against my mouth, then gently bites my lip. "I'm taking you to my bed. If you don't want that, say so now."

All I have to do is say no. One tiny little word, or even just the shake of my head, and he'll free me. I'll be safe from this overwhelming desire, from the terrible way he makes my heart stretch with his contradictions. A criminal, yes, but also someone genuinely fascinated by the human condition. A man who wears his indifference as a shield and his guilt like he's earned it.

I thought he could teach me to avoid men like him, but I'm realizing that there's no one like Cassian. And that might be the most dangerous lesson of all.

Still, I can't say no. If bad boys are my weakness, Cassian is my fatal flaw, the poison I'll adore till I die.

"I want to," I say, my voice so breathless I barely recognize it. "I want *you.*"

I mean all of him. Not just his body but his past, his secrets, the parts he never shows to anyone else. I don't ask openly for those though. He's still a playboy and a heartbreaker, and I'm not so naive to think I can change him.

But when this is over, I'll be so wrecked I'll never touch a bad boy again. I already know it. So in a way, he's already held up his end of our bargain.

He sweeps me off my feet, laughing when I gasp. "No one's ever done that before?"

"I'm just under six feet tall," I say. "I'm not the being-carried type."

He snorts as he heads for the door. "Lucky for you I'm not intimidated by tall women. In fact"—he leans close as if telling me a naughty secret—"I love them."

"You love all women." But I wrap my arm around his neck, savoring how solid he is. "How tall are you?"

"Six something. And I do not love all women." He slows, stops, his expression going serious. "Before we finish this, I need you to understand something. I'll never tell you lies. Not once. You have to tell me you understand that, or I'm stopping now."

I blink up at him. He's as deadly serious as when he was telling me about his mom. "Okay," I say hesitantly. "You're not lying."

He gives me a little shake. "No. *I've never lied to you.* Not about how fucking sexy you are, how worked up you get me, how goddamn amazing you are. Tell me you understand."

My eyes go wide as I remember everything he's ever said to me. He meant all that. It wasn't just flirting or lessons or whatever else I told myself so I could dismiss his words. I swallow hard, my heart feeling as if it's flooded. "Okay," I say again. *"You're not lying."*

His mouth compresses for a moment like he's trying to hold something in. He nods once, sharply, and then we're moving again.

He takes me to a part of the house I haven't been in before, an entire wing away from where the guest room was. The art on the walls shifts from the black-and-white photographs to vibrant watercolors of all different kinds of people. Old, young, various sexes and races, people from all over the world. The images aren't exactly flattering, but they are honest.

Before I can ask him who the artist is, Cassian's kicking open the door to a bedroom. His bedroom.

The bed isn't massive, which is the first surprise. Also, it's perfectly made up. The entire room is neat, organized. There's a small desk with a stack of books and an open notebook and a pen lying across it. More of the watercolors hang from the walls, larger than the ones in the hall.

It's not at all what I pictured, but now that I've seen it—and he's told me about his past—it fairly screams Cassian.

"No one else has seen this, have they?" I ask as he lets me down. I already know the answer though.

"Besides Lawford? No." He catches my chin, tilts my face up. "Only you."

My pulse stutters. I know he's not lying, but I also have to remind myself that this won't last. That this is for tonight and however many nights after, but not forever.

"I want to feel your bare skin on mine," I confess. Even after all our teasing, verbal and physical, I haven't gotten that and it's a crying shame.

"God, I know," he says. "I want to go slow though. You deserve slow." He gives me languid kisses all along my neck. "You deserve everything."

"Everything includes fast." I unfasten one of the buttons on his shirt, then another.

His laugh is strained. "That's true. You're so damn clever." He shrugs out of his shirt once I've reached the last button. "I can barely keep up with you."

I know he's not lying, but that's not true. He's the clever one, the one I can barely keep up with. But when he slows down for me…

I take in the sight of his bare chest, my breath trapped in my lungs. His skin is smooth, hot, and he's got the most perfect body. Not overly muscular, but *honed.* Like angels chiseled out his form in a burst of inspiration. This is what all those ancient Greek sculptors were trying to capture. Too bad they didn't have Cassian as a model.

He's already working on his pants as I stand there staring. He pushes off his boxers and pants in one move, leaving himself entirely nude. The rest of him is just as glorious. His erection is proud, firm. And his ass… I've never understood the phrase *juicy ass* until now. But I want to take a bite out of his butt it looks so good.

"Come here," he growls. "Why are you still dressed?"

"I got distracted."

"Oh?" He whips my shirt over my head. "By something good?"

Beast. He knows I was distracted by him, and he's looking for a compliment. "It was definitely an eyeful." I smirk at him.

"More than an eyeful." He's got my bra undone in under a second. "And I'll show you exactly how much more."

With a single tug, my pants and panties are gone. Goose-flesh rises all over me, not because I'm cold but because I'm so exposed and he's so close. I need him covering me.

He takes a moment to run his hands over me appreciatively. "You looked so fucking amazing in that nightgown," he says. "But you look even better out of it. This"—he skims the curve of my waist—"and this"—he continues along the lines of my thigh—"is going to be the only fantasy I'll ever have after this."

He's not lying, but I also don't think that's true. It hurts to imagine him with whoever comes after me though, so I shove the idea away. This is my time, and I'm going to savor every second.

It's definitely true for me though—he's the only fantasy I'll ever have.

He sweeps me up again. This time I can feel intimately how solid his body is, how heat radiates off him. My skin seems to sizzle where it touches his.

When he lays me on the bed, I stretch out, the better to appreciate how his gaze runs over me.

"I wanted to give you slow. But this time has to be fast. I can't wait for you any longer." His voice actually shakes when he says it, shakes so hard it has me quivering. He dips his head, takes my nipple in his mouth. He flicks with his tongue and I start to come undone, just that easy.

Maybe it's because he's just so purely delighted with me. He's touching me, loving me with his hands and mouth because he genuinely enjoys it and not because it's the price he has to pay to fuck me. He promised fast, and while I am getting dangerously close to the edge already, it also seems like he can do this forever and happily.

When his fingers find my pussy, he sucks in a breath. "So wet," he mutters. "I can never get over how wet and hot you are for me. How fucking beautifully you get aroused."

His erection is hard and hot against my hip, and even his barest touch has me desperate to have him inside me.

"Now," I moan. "I'm wet. *Now.*"

He lifts his head. "Have you ever said that before? *I'm wet?*"

I blush without meaning to. "No. I never… Dirty talk isn't my thing."

He strokes my clit, sending my thoughts scattering. "Dirty talk is definitely your thing. Do it again."

My cheeks go even hotter. "I can't. There's…"

"Whatever's in your head," he urges. "Just spill it. Like you're spilling on my hand right now."

Oh, I am. I can feel my juices—on him, on me. Can hear them even. And my clit is so swollen, so slippery.

"It feels so good," I try. "Your fingers…"

He shakes his head. "Baby, your body is saying something much filthier. Now you say it." He draws slow, maddening circles on my clit, just enough to keep the pressure on but not enough to relieve it.

"My clit…" I stammer, trip over the word. "I need more."

"Mmm." His strokes stay slow.

I grind my teeth. "Fuck," I mutter. "Fine. I need you to stroke my clit, hard and fast. I need you inside me, filling me."

He immediately rewards me, his thumb working at my clit. He slips one, two fingers inside me. "There you go, beautiful. But I think you want more."

My fists are clenched as my head thrashes from side to side. I'm close, so close to coming. But he's right. "It's right there," I pant. "But I want your cock, not your fingers."

He kisses me deep and harsh, like he's been waiting his entire life to hear that. "You've got me," he says. "All of me."

In a moment, he's got a condom on. In the next, he's filling me completely, spreading my legs to make room for him.

To be so gloriously, completely filled… The pleasure in me swells, flowing to the very tips of my fingers. He thrusts hard, his pelvis catching on my clit.

"Ung." I make a strange grunting exhale, nothing like I've done before because this is nothing like I've ever felt before. He's fast, he's losing control, but somehow with each pump of his hips, he catches on spots I didn't know I had, making sparks dance behind my eyes.

"V," he mutters, over and over again. "Jesus. God."

The pleasure takes on a rhythmic peak, flooding all my nerves. "I'm coming," I get out.

"Me too."

And then we climax together, me pulsing around him as he pulses into me.

It's so perfect in that moment; I almost believe that it can last forever.

CHAPTER 17

When I wake up, I realize two things.

It's dark, which means I slept the entire afternoon away, which is something I never do. And I've got Victoria wrapped around me, which means I fell asleep with her in the bed, which is also something I never do.

For all that I give my lovers what they need, I've never been one to linger. I'll cuddle as long as they want, but falling asleep together? Not my thing.

I don't want to get up though. Victoria's hair is out of her ponytail and spread over my chest, her breathing is deep and even and tangled in my own, and her limbs are the sweetest weights holding me down.

I can get used to this. Sleeping like this, waking up like this. I know this is only supposed to be instructive for Victoria, but… it can be more. Maybe.

Dwelling on the future is too much right now though. I want to savor the present. And the past some too—I've never had sex like that before. Oh, it's been good—really fucking good—but to have a woman's climax touch me inside, like right on my freaking heart? No. That hasn't happened.

Her eyes flutter open, slow and soft, like something out of

a fairy tale. She gives a little start when she realizes she's draped over me, then relaxes again.

"Am I smashing you?" she asks without moving. It sounds like she's as content as I am.

"No." I run my hand over her hair. "I'm good. You?"

She fills her lungs, nibbles on her lip. "Yeah. This is good." She walks her fingers across my chest. "I hate your Instagram."

I laugh in disbelief. "Okay. What made you think of that?"

"Your Instagram is very sexy."

"Thank you," I say dryly.

Her fingers give me a little pinch. "It's sexy, but it's fake. I like it when you're real."

"It's not fake," I say. "It's the brand. People want to buy things from someone they can aspire to be, not someone who's real. Reality's overrated."

She lifts her head. "Oh really?"

"Well, not this." I caress her arm. "This reality is excellent. But it's not for Instagram. Unless…"

She pinches me again. "I know you're teasing, so I won't respond."

"You pinched me," I point out. "Also, you never told me what your Instagram handle is. I couldn't figure it out from my follower list."

It was a bitch and a half to go through the 1.5 million accounts that follow me, and it was especially frustrating to not find her account there. I even started searching my likes to see if she would pop up.

"I don't follow you," she says primly. "I told you, I don't like your account."

I tuck my arms behind my head and grin at her. "But you stalk it anyway. So tell me, what's your Instagram handle? I promise I won't follow back."

My follow list is very carefully curated. Following her

account would bring way too much unwanted attention to her. I'll have to follow her from my private burner account.

She rolls her eyes, then reaches for her phone on the bedside table. "I warn you, it's boring."

My pulse picks up in spite of that. She's finally going to show me. And while she might think it's boring, it's also hers, which means I'll be fascinated no matter what.

"I promise not to be interested." I sit up, the better to see.

She hands over the phone. The grid is all… "Dogs?" I frown. "Holy shit, how many dogs do you own? How do you take care of them all?"

She laughs into her hand. "Oh my God, they're not all mine! I'm not a hoarder. They're foster animals. Dogs looking for a home."

I check her follower numbers. It's more than decent for a nonmonetized account. "So you volunteer at the shelter and post pictures of the dogs?"

Her mouth twists. "Well, it's more than that." The hesitation in her voice cuts at me. There's more, stuff she doesn't want to tell me. "The program, it's for foster kids too. Saturday mornings they come and work with the dogs. But I can't show the kids on the feed for privacy reasons. I can't even talk much about them, because people get these weird ideas, like they can pick up a kid along with the dog. And the point of foster care is reunification." She wrings her hands like she's just now realized she's babbling. "It's a good program, but there're parts I have to keep quiet about for the sake of the kids."

Slowly I lower the phone. This was why she got so upset about my setting up the fake animal charity. I'm tempted to tell her about the foundation I started, but I also don't want to detract from any of this, because what she's doing is remarkable.

"You help dogs and kids," I say. "And you don't want anyone to know about it."

"I mean, I want people to know about the dogs so they can find a home." She lets her hands drop, then crosses her arms. "But I don't want them to know it's me."

"Right. Why would you want to take credit for the good you do?" I shake my head because it's so painfully like her. "I won't say anything, but I'm not going to pretend that you're not amazing for doing this."

She snatches her phone back. "Someone had to."

That's probably true, but I doubt anyone else would have. "It's a good thing," I say. "More people should be like you."

She shifts, looks down. Her hand snakes out and grabs the sheet, tucking it under her arms, covering her.

Shit. I said something wrong, but I can't figure out what it was.

"It feels…" Her mouth tenses. "I know it's important. But after everything, it feels like not enough. Like I'm letting everyone down by not being… being what I should have."

Meaning an officer in the Army. But I don't buy that's what she should have been. I kiss her hand. "You're exactly what you're supposed to be. Brave, loyal, kind, dutiful." I kiss her again. "Beautiful." Another kiss. "Sexy."

Her smile is sad. "Yeah, they don't teach those last things at West Point. And you said it yourself—why am I working for someone else and not running my own company?"

I wince as she tosses my careless words back at me. "I'm an idiot. You shouldn't listen to me."

"You're not and you're right. I can't work for Tess forever. I mean, I love her and she's my best friend, but the job is only… it's a holding pattern because I'm too afraid to do anything else."

"Anyone who works with dogs and kids isn't afraid. Not of anything. And if that's your passion, you're smart enough to build something around that. So do it."

"I guess…" She chews on her lip. "I guess I'm afraid I'll

ruin it, just like I did my Army career. And then the kids will be hurt."

"I understand." And I do, because my failures have hurt the people I care about the most. I won't give her any empty platitudes about how that won't happen.

She meets my eyes with a grateful expression. "Someday I'll be ready to risk again. I just… I don't know when that is."

She's so open, so vulnerable, it makes my throat ache. She has no idea how brave she really is. "I know you will," I say. "I never had any doubts about that. If you need anything when you do…"

It feels odd to be offering her money and support—we're beyond that kind of stuff it seems—but it's also all I have to give her. I mean, I can set up a marketing campaign too. But she'll need a company first.

Her smile is wry, prepping me for her gentle rejection. "Thanks. But I think the bargain we have now is enough."

Except it isn't, at least not for me. But given the circumstances, I can't tell her that.

CHAPTER 18

I used to think I could live with a guilty conscience. After all, I did it for five years up until now. I can do it for the rest of my life if I need to.

After telling Victoria about my past, all the awful, horrible things I've done, suddenly I can't do it anymore. My guilt grew into a canker, painful, throbbing. It's been two days since I saw her last, and I haven't been able to sleep.

So today I invited Oscar over. Raven knows and Morgan knows, but that isn't enough. They aren't the only people we wronged.

I'm going to tell Oscar everything today. I didn't tell the other guys I'm doing it, mostly because I don't want them to talk me out of it. Not that they can.

Confessing the truth is what Victoria would do. The right thing to do. And I'm going to do it. All on my own.

I'm waiting for Oscar in the library, my stomach tied into flinty knots as I sip the bourbon I poured myself. Bane is a shadow prowling the shelves, slinking through some leather-bound classics, winding his way through my college computer science texts. I'll know when Oscar arrives because Bane will disappear. He always knows before anyone else when someone comes.

My notebook from Ira sits on the side table. I have no urge to look through it. Just having it here is irritating me—why couldn't Ira have left us something normal and not a damn puzzle to solve? Why is Tynan playing these exact same games?

Perhaps I don't have the right to be angry with them, not after what I did. But I still am.

Bane gives a plaintive meow, startling me out of my thoughts. He almost never makes any kind of noise, so his thready, rattling cry is unfamiliar. And a little eerie.

"What is it?" I ask, as if he can actually tell me.

He looks out the window where the sun is setting over the trees surrounding the house. He meows again, louder this time, as if there's something I have to see.

But there's nothing there. Still, I keep staring out in case I'm missing something.

Then Bane whirls around and is out of the room in a flash. I blink once, and he's gone.

Which must mean Oscar's here.

Sure enough, Lawford shows him in a few minutes later. Oscar looks tired, older than he should. As if time caught up with him, then piled on another decade too.

"You feeling all right?" I ask as he takes a chair.

Oscar lowers himself slowly. "Just tired. No, not even tired. Just old." His smile is threadbare.

This suddenly seems like a terrible idea. What if the shock of my confession kills him? I know logically that's not likely to happen—bad news doesn't cause heart attacks, arterial blockages do—but I still want to protect him from the impact.

"You should get more rest," I say. "Enjoy your retirement."

"Oh, am I retired?" He's joking, but it feels brittle.

"No, but you should retire. Take some time for yourself finally." I lift the bottle of bourbon to offer some to him.

He shakes his head. "I have to drive." His smile is a touch sad. "I'm paranoid about those things."

It hits me like a fist to the gut. Of course he would be. "Sure." I set the bottle down, take a moment. This is going to be much harder than I thought.

Something from the corner of the room catches my eye, a shadow moving within a shadow. I'd swear that it's Bane, but there's no way he's still in here.

"What did you want to talk about?" Oscar asks. "You sounded concerned on the phone."

I clear my throat, turn back to him. "Yeah. There's been some…" My faculty with words starts to fail me. Me, who can talk anyone into anything, and I can't seem to speak right now.

It's the right thing to do.

That comes in Victoria's voice, her hard, implacable officer's tone. My little tin soldier, reminding me to straighten up, to do my duty.

I take a long drink from my bourbon, mostly to give myself a moment to retrieve my words. "Do you remember the self-driving system we were working on?" I ask quietly.

Oscar's face sags for a moment. "I do. I wondered why you never followed up on that—it had great commercial potential. But then with Ira…" He shrugs, but the gesture is slow, pained.

He probably thinks we abandoned the project for the same reason he's careful about drinking and driving. When your best friend dies in a car wreck, you never look at driving the same way again.

I sit across from him, settling my elbows against my knees. "Oscar, Ira's death wasn't an accident."

Now that I've said it, there's no going back. It doesn't feel good exactly, but it does feel right.

Oscar goes white. Very, very white. "What do you mean?" His tone grates against my ears.

"We had the self-driving system in his car." I force myself to hold Oscar's gaze, to not look away from what I've done. "It was running when they crashed. It might have been responsible for the crash."

My mouth is dry, my heart is pounding, but I get all that out without hesitation. Again, it doesn't feel good, but it does feel right.

Oscar has gone still. Stone still. If his chest wasn't moving with his breaths, he might be a statue. "Why would you think that?" His voice is whisper quiet.

"Because someone delivered the self-driving system to me. The exact one that we built. The one that was in the car that night."

His mouth opens, but nothing comes out. He looks like he might be struggling for breath.

"Oscar." I start to get up. "Are you all right? Should I call—"

He waves me off. "I just need a moment. Who sent it to you?"

I watch him carefully. He seems to be recovering. "We think it was Tynan."

He stands up suddenly, his hands trembling. "Tynan's alive? That can't be." He's almost furious in his disbelief. "Where the fuck is he?"

That catches me up. Oscar never swears. Shit. He's so upset he's cussing.

"We don't know," I say calmly. Maybe I was right to be worried about the whole heart attack thing. "We're not even sure he's alive. We're only assuming. It makes the most sense that he'd be behind the attempted theft of the notebook and sending me the computer."

Oscar's gaze flicks to the side table. There's an emotion close to hatred in his eyes and what looks like greed when he spots the notebook. But then he rubs his hand over his face, his shoulders slumping, and the impression is entirely gone.

"This is a hard thing to hear," he says from behind his hand. "Ira was my best friend."

"I know. We… we never knew for certain that the computer was running when they crashed. We assumed that it wasn't, mostly to avoid blaming ourselves. And that was wrong."

Oscar's hand drops. "Did you recover the drives? Have you run it again?"

"The operating system was still intact, but not the recorded data," I say. "So we really have no idea what happened. It hasn't thrown an error in all the test data we've given it. And we even replicated the conditions of the road the night Ira died. The system behaves exactly as it should."

He lowers himself back into his chair. He stares off at nothing. "No errors," he mutters to himself. "Then how…?"

"We don't know," I say. "But we're still testing. The next step is to put it back into a car."

He nods jerkily. "Of course. But that's dangerous."

"We have to find out what happened. We owe it to Ira. And to Tynan."

"Yes." He looks as if he's still trying to puzzle out what all this means. "Yes, you'll have to do that. Investigate everything."

His color is still bad. But at least he hasn't collapsed.

"We will," I assure him. "We know we're responsible and… well, we can't make it right, but we can at least find our mistake. And maybe even convince Tynan to come back to us. I should show you what we have so far. Maybe you'll see something we missed."

"You shouldn't be telling me about all this." Oscar's expression is gently self-mocking. "I don't understand any of it."

He's selling himself short, as usual.

"You were Ira's partner too," I remind him. "Those advances in neuronal interfaces—those were yours too."

Out of everything I've said, that seems to hit him the hardest, pulling all the remaining vitality out of him. He stares at his hands for a long moment. So long I start to worry all over again.

"Oscar?"

When he looks up, his gaze is haunted. With effort, he brings his expression back under control, blinking several times.

"If you..." Shit, I'm losing my words again. "If you can't get past this, I understand. *We* understand. Morgan... I don't think she can. Not really."

He stares at me for a moment. "No." He shakes his head. "No, it was an accident. You boys would never hurt Ira. Not intentionally."

"But we did." I don't even have to force that out, although my voice is quiet. "We did."

Oscar reaches over, clasps my shoulder. The weight of his hand... I feel like my heart could crack under that weight.

"It wasn't your fault." His voice is steady, comforting. "You didn't mean for this to happen. Didn't mean for anyone to get hurt."

"Our intentions don't matter. We're still guilty."

His expression sharpens. "Have you told anyone else about this?"

"We weren't even going to tell Raven and Morgan at first."

He nods sagely. "Good. Keep it to yourselves. I don't want any of you to go to prison over this."

"Even if we deserve it?"

His hand tightens on my shoulder. "You don't. And you should have told me sooner. You know this doesn't change how I see you all."

Relief spreads through me. After everything that's happened with my family, to have lost Oscar too... "Thanks," I say huskily.

"You just promise me one thing."

"Anything."

For a moment his eyes glimmer with emotion. "Promise me you'll be careful when you put that thing back into a car. I can't lose you too."

Fuck. Okay, now I *really* can't talk. But I won't let myself cry. "Sure." I clear my throat. "Don't worry about me. I'll be fine."

Especially now that I've unburdened myself to him and he hasn't turned his back on me.

CHAPTER 19

"Absolutely not," Cassian roars, setting down the tool he was using. "Stop asking, because it will never happen."

He looks to the rest of the guys standing around the car as if to appeal to them for help with me. They all look away, tucking their hands into their pockets. *Not my fight* their postures say.

Cassian sighs and turns back to me. "Baby."

My eyebrows shoot up into my hairline as Gideon clears his throat. Loudly.

Cassian rolls his eyes. "Okay, Lieutenant Shepherd."

"She's not in the Army anymore," Gage points out.

I nod, keeping my arms crossed over my chest. I don't bother to point out that I was actually a captain when I left the service. He can yell all he wants, but I'm not budging. It's nowhere near as dangerous as he says, and I can't let him do this alone. It goes against my every instinct as a former officer and as a person.

And as someone who cares very deeply for him.

"I'm not afraid," I point out.

Cassian looks as if he's torn between the urge to kiss me and strangle me. "I know you're not. That's entirely my point. You should be afraid. If anything happens to you…"

He shakes his head, going back to installing the self-driving system on the car. "I forbid it. The subject is closed."

A look passes between all the rest of the guys. The five of them are assembled to help Cassian and me install the AI on a car so that we can do road testing. All of them came around quickly to my theory that only in the road testing would the true error come out.

But when I said I wanted to be in the car for the test, Cassian lost his mind. I knew he'd be upset, but I didn't imagine he'd lose his cool. Especially in front of everyone.

It looks like everyone else didn't expect this from him either.

"I don't think you can tell her what to do," Archer says. His face is impassive, but I get the impression he's laughing inside.

Gideon starts to say something, then stops. Then starts again, stops again. He seems to want to agree with Cassian that I shouldn't go but also sees that Cassian really doesn't have any standing to tell me no.

Except for the fact that it's his system and his car. But I agreed to help him, and I've helped install it all. So I have some ownership here.

"Is there something you want to share?" Bishop asks Gideon.

Gideon sighs, rubs his hands over his face. "If anything happens to you," he says to me, "Tess will be crushed."

"But Cassian can just die?" I glare at them.

They all shift guiltily.

"No, of course not," Gideon says. "But this isn't your problem. Or your risk to take."

Cassian stops what he's doing. "See? We're all in agreement."

I put my hands on my hips. "I only hear you and Gideon. And you're both biased. Also, Archer thinks you can't tell me what to do."

"Archer thinks wrong." Cassian is so far from his usual I-don't-give-a-shit attitude it's like he's a different person.

My gaze swings to Bishop. "What do you think?"

He takes a long moment before answering. "It isn't your problem. Cassian—or one of us—should be the one behind the wheel, taking on the danger. But if you insist, I won't stop you."

"And if it was Raven asking to go?" Cassian's eyes glitter dangerously.

Bishop's mouth compresses. "I'd tell her the same. I don't command her."

Cassian looks as if he'd like to continue and say something nasty. But he catches my eye and stops. "Can we just finish putting this in?" He sounds weary. "And maybe fight about this later?"

"I like that idea," Gideon says too eagerly.

The rest of them look relieved, so I let it drop. We can argue about it later, and we will. For now we need to get going so we can test it here in Cassian's driveway.

Cassian told me he got an old car similar to Ira's that we can test it in. He assured me it wouldn't be anything anyone would miss. But the car turned out to be a lovingly kept Mercedes from the eighties, riding that fine line between being coolly retro and simply out of date.

Gage runs a hand along the car's fender. "Oscar really gave this to you?"

I look up in surprise from the cable I'm connecting to the steering column. "This is from Oscar?"

Cassian nods. "He wanted to help."

"Wait." Gideon holds up a hand. "Did you tell him what it was for?"

Cassian squares his shoulders and faces them all. "I told him everything."

My mouth drops open. He never told me he was going to do that. But why should he? He doesn't owe me anything.

And even if he did feel he owes me, he still wouldn't say. He'd wait until after he did the right thing before mentioning it. He wouldn't want me to give him credit for something he hadn't done, even if he was intending to do it.

"I thought we weren't telling Oscar," Bishop says carefully. "Did the plan change?"

"What plan?" Cassian asks. "After Ira died, we hardly discussed anything. We just shoved everything under the rug in order to protect our own asses. We told Raven and Morgan—well, Oscar was hurt just as bad by Ira's death. So why shouldn't he know?"

There's no anger in Cassian—or rather, it's cool anger. Controlled. Completely unlike his reaction when I suggested I go with him on the test.

"What did he say?" Archer asks. "Because we've already lost Morgan. We might be losing Raven. Have we lost Oscar?"

"No. Not at all."

All of them are visibly relieved.

"So what did he say?" Archer asks again.

Cassian's face softens. "That whatever happened wasn't intentional. That he didn't want any of us to go to jail over this."

There's a beat of silence. Gage and Archer lower their heads.

"Oscar was always good to us," Bishop finally says.

"Not as good as Ira." That from Gideon isn't challenging —it's more a reminder of what they've all lost.

I suddenly feel very, very out of place. I clear my throat and edge toward the house.

Cassian immediately sees me do it. "Let's finish this," he says to the rest of them. "We can be sad together later."

I almost laugh, because it's so bleak and dark and still funny. "You can be sad together," I say. "I just figured you guys wouldn't want me to watch."

"You can watch anytime," Cassian says with a glint of his old wickedness.

I roll my eyes, partly because he's ridiculous and partly because I know it will make him feel better. "Please, no. And can I go with you to test it on the road?"

"No." He turns back to finish installing the self-driving system.

I work on finishing my own part, along with all the rest of them. There's little talking except for requests for tools or confirmation that this or that is done. It's enjoyable, actually, to get my hands dirty working on this. And the guys haven't forgotten how to deal with hardware, which is unusual for tech billionaires. Some of those CEOs can't even turn on their desktop machine anymore.

"We're ready," Cassian announces after an hour or so.

I look up from the connection I'm double-checking. "Really?"

Out of nowhere, my heart starts to race. Cassian's going to let the computer drive this car while he's in it. If something happens and he gets hurt, I'll have to watch the entire thing. There won't be anything I can do from the sidelines.

It's as heart wrenching as when I had to send my people into danger. More so, actually.

Cassian catches my expression. His jaw tightens. "You really want to do this, don't you?"

"You think?" Gideon mutters. "What gave it away?"

I chew on my lip. "I know I'm not as invested as the rest of you, but I am involved. I can't let you do this alone."

Cassian sighs like he's going to empty his lungs and never refill them. "You care too damn much."

Maybe I do. But I can't help it.

"Fine," he says shortly. "You can ride with me here in the driveway. And that's it."

"She can get hurt here too," Bishop says.

"It'll be fine." Archer looks over the car again.

Cassian looks to Gideon. Gideon shrugs. "Tess loves her, and I love Tess. So don't do anything stupid."

"Too late for that." Cassian opens the passenger door for me. "Hear that? You have to stay safe so Gideon doesn't get yelled at tonight."

"That's not—"

Cassian slams the door on Gideon's protest, and I hide my smile.

"Tess would do more than yell at him," I say as Cassian slides into the driver's seat.

"Then let's make sure she doesn't." His expression is grim as he stares straight ahead. Eventually he starts the engine. It catches with a quiet, almost hesitant cough. The self-driving system's screen lights up, asking if we'd like to engage the system.

I wait for Cassian to turn it on. He doesn't.

"I'm going to make sure we didn't break anything vital," he says, putting the car in gear. He rolls down both our windows. "The test isn't valid if we've fucked up the car in other ways."

I don't think we have, but I understand why he wants to wait. My own pulse is hammering hard inside me, driven by adrenaline and anxiety. My palms are damp and hot and my skin is flushed and tight. Taking a minute before we turn on the computer is probably a good idea if he's feeling even a little bit like I am.

We pull away from the garage, Cassian handling the car with ease. If he's nervous, it's not coming out. Mostly he looks grim.

The end of the driveway appears, the gate shut tight. It doesn't open as we approach. Instead, Cassian stops before it, then backs all the way up the driveway, reversing just as fast as he drove down the driveway. It's an impressive piece of driving, and he's confident and cool the entire time.

When we arrive back at the garage, Gage says dryly, "You survived. Congrats."

"That wasn't the test." Cassian isn't amused. He flicks on the system with a decisive tap of his fingers. "This is."

As he programs the route into the system, the white noise of anxiety in me goes quiet. The mission has started and I need to focus—so I do, calling on all my old training.

"Ready?" he asks quietly. "You can still get out."

"I won't." My tone is as steady as his. "We're doing this together."

His jaw sets, hard as steel. But he activates the program, then lifts his hands from the wheel.

It starts to turn on its own. It's so eerie I almost gasp.

"Yeah, it looks weird," Cassian says. "I never quite got used to it."

My heart has decided to stutter instead of beat, but I manage to keep my breathing steady. The car slides down the driveway, the steering wheel jerking this way and that as it tries to keep us on the pavement.

We're only going about five miles an hour, which feels agonizingly slow. Like the car is creeping along.

"Should we be going faster?" I ask. He did on our first run.

"Next time."

The gate appears, still shut. I hold my breath as we approach. The car doesn't slow down. The computer chimes occasionally at us, as if to say everything is just peachy.

The gate gets closer and closer. If we don't slow down… If it doesn't open…

If it does open, we'll be in the middle of the street.

"If you hit the brakes, will it take control from the computer?" My voice is only a touch shaky. I should have asked this before I got in the car.

"Of course." Cassian's hands are still hovering over the steering wheel, ready to seize it in a moment.

We return to tense silence. The gate keeps coming. And coming.

I set my jaw. We'll be fine. And if it crashes, then we won't be hurt and the gate can be fixed. And we'll have an error, if not *the* error.

Then, smoother than any human can do, the car starts to brake. It stops so close to the gate I'm shocked I don't hear the faint ting of the wrought iron tapping the bumper.

Everything in me that was clenched tight releases. I take a full, deep, cool breath. "That's close."

His mouth quirks humorlessly. "I forgot about that. We programmed it to do that, to show off."

"It got my attention."

The screen flashes, and then suddenly the car is backing up. It goes up the drive only slightly less smoothly than Cassian did and comes to stop in the exact same spot we started from.

The guys gather around us. Their expressions are torn between relief and triumph.

"It still works," Bishop says, a hint of giddiness running through his words.

"Yeah, in the simplest kind of test." Archer isn't so excited. He crosses his arms. "You going to do it again?"

Cassian nods. "Faster this time."

My heart kicks up.

Archer nods. "Well, keep being careful."

Cassian starts to reprogram the route. "Remember what we put in for the allowed stopping distance?"

Gage nods, and then his eyes widen. "Shit. We might have cut that one too close."

"You think?" Cassian finishes with the program. "Watch out."

The guys pull back at his warning. As soon as they're clear, the car takes off. So fast that I'm pushed back into my seat.

This time we're not playing it safe. The wheels whine, threatening to scream as we take a corner. I'm pulled against the seat belt by the centrifugal force, the straps cutting deep into my hips and shoulder.

Suddenly I'm very aware of how Cassian has no control over the car. His feet aren't on the brake or the accelerator; his hands only hover over the wheel, which is jerking back and forth. All I can think of is HAL, that evil computer from the movie, and his awful monotone, of how he killed all those people in the cold vacuum of space.

We're being driven by HAL.

I know it's not true and Cassian can take over at any moment—heck, I can shut it down myself with a tap of the screen—but I can't shake the thought. Or the cold shivers running down my spine along with the damp sweat.

The gate's coming up fast. Too fast. The car's still accelerating.

I grab my seat belt, wishing it was a five-point harness. Cassian's hands sink another inch toward the wheel. His face is pale, his expression grim.

The gate keeps coming. I brace for impact even though I know Cassian won't let us crash.

I'm thrown forward against the seat belt before I even register that the car has started to brake. The wheels scream this time, the smell of burning brake dust and rubber filling the air.

Without thinking, I glance down. Cassian's foot isn't near the brake. The car is doing this entirely on its own.

This time we stop even closer to the gate, crashing back into the seats as the car slams to a full halt.

I suck in as much air as I can past my tight throat. "Holy—"

The car snaps into reverse, roaring backward up the drive even faster than we came down. My heart is going so fast I can't hear individual beats anymore. It's just one sustained thump.

I turn in my seat to watch. The guys are where we left them, only more wide-eyed now. As we come racing into the garage area, they all step back.

Except for Gage. At the last possible moment, he steps directly into the path of the car. Right where it should stop.

I yelp.

"Shit," Cassian hisses. His foot stomps down, reaching for the brake, trying to stop the car.

It keeps going.

It's too late for Gage to get out of the way. Too late for us to brake.

Except, somehow, the car does. The wheels lock up, sending the car into a skid. The wheel jerks wildly on its own, the computer trying to correct for it.

We seem to slide endlessly, helplessly, right into where Gage is standing. Until suddenly the car stops, the entire frame heaving as momentum catches up with us.

I blink, gasp, hardly daring to look. But I do.

Gage is standing behind the car, his face pale. But he looks untouched. Slowly he lowers his palms to the lid of the trunk.

"Jesus," Cassian murmurs. Then louder, angrier, "*Jesus. What the fuck were you thinking?*"

I dimly register that the proximity alarm has been screeching the entire time.

"Fuck," Cassian says again, mostly to himself. "You okay?"

I nod. My chest floods with relief that I'm still alive. That Gage is still alive. "It worked?"

Cassian rakes his fingers through his hair before he shuts down the computer, then turns off the car. "Yes. At least it did that time."

Gideon opens my door and offers me his hand. "That

was…" He swallows hard. "It worked." He's got a bright note of triumph there peeking out.

Cassian's the opposite of triumphant. "We don't want it to work. We need it to fail." His gaze runs over me. "But next time though, when it's just me."

He swings out of the car with furious grace, leaving me to be helped by Gideon. The rest of them cluster around us. Gage has regained his color.

"You shouldn't have done that," Cassian says.

I have to agree—I'm going to have nightmares about Gage stepping into the path of the car for sure.

"You wanted a test." Gage shrugs. "Maybe someone stepped out into the road, the car swerved, and…"

Even as he says it, he knows it's not what happened. All this mystery and intrigue for the car simply swerving off the road? No, something more must have happened, something that Tynan needs Cassian to figure out.

I look at Archer and wonder what's happening with the notebooks. Cassian hasn't kept me updated on what more Archer might have found using the note tucked inside the computer case. Either they've found nothing or I'm not important enough to be kept in the loop.

"It's not supposed to just swerve," Bishop says. "It has to assess the environment, see if that's the best course."

"And it did," Archer says. "If it had swerved, it would have hit you. It came to a hard stop."

Hard enough to leave deep black skid marks on the driveway. They look like they're never coming out.

Gage shrugs. "Okay, so it still works. Mostly. Now what?"

"We have to take it out there. To the exact spot." Cassian's voice is stark, stripped to the bone.

No one says anything. Probably because we all knew this was coming. Was always coming.

I knew it the moment the idea came to me to test the car in real-world conditions.

I grab Cassian's arm. "Not tonight." I can't explain how waiting will help anything, but the urge to stop him is overwhelming. "Can we just wait until tomorrow?"

He shakes his head. "Not *we*. Only me. There's no way you're going with me to that spot to do this." His expression softens. "But yeah, we'll wait." For a brief moment he reaches up, touches my cheek.

And in that moment, I can almost believe that tomorrow's test will be fine.

I should be excited that the first test today went so well. Instead, all I can feel is a gathering dread.

The computer is fucked. It looks and behaves as if it isn't, but deep within, there's a fatal error. And the more I keep pushing, the closer I come to it, until one time that error's going to lash out and catch me, the same as it did Ira and Tynan.

It could even happen tomorrow. It should, if my guess is correct and the computer was programmed to kill them.

Thank God Victoria won't be there when it happens.

She's sitting next to me on the couch, curled into me. We haven't said much since the guys left and Lawford ordered us in some dinner. Somehow we both know she's staying the night. After that…

I run my hands down her back, her sides, savoring her warmth, her curves, how she melts into me. I knew she would be gorgeous when she unwound. I just didn't know how gorgeous. How devastating.

She wanted me to teach her how to avoid men like me, but she's ruined every other woman for me. After this, she's likely to find some nice guy, the one she always wanted. And she'll forever be the one *I* always wanted.

A deep, sharp jealousy stabs me right in the chest at the thought. But I've got her tonight, so this mystery future guy can stuff it.

"Let's go to bed," I whisper in her ear.

As soon as the bedroom door closes behind us, Victoria starts kissing me with a desperate intensity.

I capture her wrists, pull back. "Slow down. We've got all night."

Her expression is stark. "But just tonight. Tomorrow the car will throw the error when you test it. And then our bargain is done."

My heart sinks, because she might be right. If we do see the error, I'm going be consumed with tracking it down, figuring out what went wrong and where, and what Tynan's trying to tell me. It wouldn't be fair to ask her to stick around through that.

"But it might not." Suddenly some deep corner of my heart wants the error to never happen again. Then she'll have to stay. "It's just as possible that it won't. That whatever happened was a one-off thing, a tragedy never to be repeated."

"If you really believe that, then why can't I come with you?"

"Because if anything happened to you…" My voice fails as I realize that losing her would be even worse than losing Ira. A thousand times worse.

I buried my father when I lost Ira. I'd bury my heart and soul if I lost her.

"You'll be ready this time." It's like she's arguing for some-thing deeper. Beyond the self-driving-system test.

"I might be," I say. "But I need it to throw this error. And when it does… things get way more complicated. I don't want you in the middle of it."

She looks like she wants to argue. Like she wants to set that pretty jaw of hers and annihilate my resistance. She can do it too, given enough time. Wear down my armor until she reaches my heart. And then all she has to do is reach in and take it.

Instead, she dips her head to kiss me. I'm both relieved and disappointed. My heart isn't worth shit, but it would have been nice to have her fight for it.

I kiss her back, guiding her toward the bed as I do. Any moment where she's not naked, where I'm not inside her, is a tragic waste. I only have tonight, and I'm going to take it and her to the utmost limits. Along with myself.

"Tell me what you want," I say the moment we hit the bed together. She's under me, completely enclosed by me. "I know there're some filthy fantasies going on behind those green eyes."

She doesn't even hesitate. "Your mouth on my pussy. Your tongue inside me, fucking me."

Jesus, that does sound good. My cock goes rock hard.

I make a noncommittal noise because she can give me more than that. "You're missing out on a lot." I pull her shirt over her head, then take off her bra. She's got the most exquisite breasts—high, firm, the perfect size for my palms. I cup them, savoring the feel. "There's so much more of you that you're forgetting. Like here." I roll her nipples between my fingers.

She throws her head back. "Oh yes."

I tug. "Oh yes, what? Come on, let that dirty tongue of yours tell me."

"You're merciless," she pants out.

"I am," I agree mildly. "But it's all for you."

"Suck on them." She throws that out like a dare. "Hard. But no teeth."

"You might like my teeth." But I do exactly as she commanded, teasing her nipples to tight, aching points.

She's bucking under me, moaning with each flick of my tongue. My cock is pulsing in time with her noises, straining against my pants. I haven't been this close to exploding while fully dressed since… ever.

"You could come just from this, couldn't you?" I ask with wonder. "God, so fucking responsive. So fucking…"

I can't find the words to tell her how awed I am by her, that it's a gift to be the man who sees her like this. Who can bring her to this point.

I guess that's how stunning she is—she can make me, the silver-tongued genius, speechless. Since I can't find words, I decide to find a better use for my mouth and slide down her body until I'm between her legs, right at eye level with her spectacular pussy.

I inhale the scent of her arousal, musky, sharp, and a thunderbolt moves through me. I have to press my face into her thigh and take a moment, otherwise I'll be slamming into her in the next second. She comes undone more beautifully than any other woman I've ever known. Or ever will again.

"V." I say it into her soft skin, test the resiliency of her thighs with my teeth. She gives a stuttering moan, moving like a living wave under me. She's completely surrendered to what's about to happen.

So I taste her, every inch, every fold, every sweet, secret spot. Her clit is the most perfect pearl, her folds richer than rose petals. But best of all is how she's moving with my mouth, my tongue, how she's letting go of every noise building in her, holding back nothing.

"I'm going to come." Her voice is as liquid as her movements, but with the sharp hitch of a rising peak. "I'm going to come so hard."

I can taste it in her juices, the subtle shift. Her legs tighten around me, such sweet, hard pressure. Her hips jerk, and I feel the fluttering contractions under my tongue.

Raising my head, I watch her expression as the climax washes over her. Just the purest, soft bliss. And I brought her to that. Or at least helped bring her to that. A lot of it was pure Victoria.

When she opens her eyes, she stares straight at me and says, "I need more."

"Jesus." An orgasm like that and she wants more? How can I ever let go of this woman? I rear up on my knees, run a hand over my aching cock. "I've got so much more ready for you."

She follows me, climbing up onto her elbows. Then she's tearing open my pants, telling me to hurry, hurry, in sounds that are less than words. I get the condom on, not needing her encouragement to be quick.

In the next moment, she's under me and I'm inside her. I can't move for a minute because it's…

For this instant, it feels as if I can be a man worthy of being with her, inside her, when her body welcomes me like this. And then the animal in me takes over, driving into her, seeking the relief, the release only she can give me.

Still I watch her and her reactions, seeking the angle, the speed, the twist that will please her most. My world shrinks down to her, expands to everything that is her.

She turns her head into the pillow, lifts her fist to her mouth to bite it. At the same time, she clenches around me, her second climax coming on.

It's too goddamn beautiful and abandoned to resist. So I let her and my climax conquer me.

We collapse together in a damp, panting heap. My brain can only register sensations for a long time—heated skin, soft breath, tangled hair across my chest.

As my thoughts come back, so does an oppressive realization—I have to let her go. I can't let her be endangered by my stupid decisions. This is way beyond scamming people out of money or a jail sentence. Hell, I'd welcome those at this point.

"I'm taking you home after this." My voice is almost

steely, although my hand on her back is gentle. I'm bracing for her argument, readying myself to fight for something I don't want.

She stiffens against me. And then slowly, as if against her will, relaxes. "I knew this was coming."

The sadness in her voice almost undoes me. "We both did. There was always an expiration date on this."

She might think I mean our bargain where I teach her all my tricks. But what I really mean is what's grown between us, the thing that's too real for any of my lessons or manipulations.

For a moment she buries her face in my chest, her nose against my sternum, her breath hot and fast against my skin. I set my hand on her hair, holding her close.

Then she raises her head, her eyes dry, her expression set. "I'll get my clothes then."

I don't tell her not to, although my heart does, silently. Too quiet for her to hear. Too quiet to stop her.

CHAPTER 21

We're driving in complete silence. I suppose because there's nothing more to say.

Cassian's going to try to get a computer to attempt to kill him tomorrow, and I'm going to... I don't know what I'll do. I should go to work, load more dog pictures to Instagram, call my parents, hang out with Tess off the clock. All the things I've let slide since I met Cassian. It would be pointless to do nothing while I wait to hear what happens with him.

But that's probably what I'll do. I can already tell I'll be useless until I hear he's safe.

"You'll call me?" My question sounds too loud in the heavy quiet. "After?"

He steers the car through a tight turn. On the massive screen in the console, the car flashes a brief warning—*Anti-skid Engaged.* The Inspiron is a nagging kind of car, beeping when you haven't fastened your seat belt fast enough, chiming when you've gone over the speed limit, squawking when you go a hair out of your lane. It aggressively wants to keep you safe, like a demented robot nanny.

Cassian isn't driving recklessly—he's as controlled and smooth as ever—but there's an edge to every motion he makes. I understand, because I'm on that same edge. Maybe the car is somehow picking up on that. Morgan was probably smart enough to put that into the car's AI.

"Of course." His jaw is so tight it barely moves as he speaks. "I won't leave you in the dark."

No, he wouldn't. But soon enough his life will return to how it used to be, and I'll torment myself by looking at his Instagram and seeing him go back to simply being Cassian the brand. Not the Cassian I got to know.

I'm not sure if I'll be masochistic enough to follow him on the gossip sites. He's not going to spend the rest of his life alone—he certainly hasn't up until now. Seeing him with whatever beautiful person fits his brand at the moment…

I blow out a long, shaky breath, my heart shuddering at the thought.

"It will be okay," Cassian says. "Tomorrow. Everything will be fine."

He misunderstood what I'm upset about. But I'm also upset about that. "Are the guys going with you? In case…"

He nods too fast, as if he can ease my hurt with the force of his agreement. "They'll be right there. And you'll be safe, which is the most important part."

It isn't the most important part to me. But I let it go. "Good." The *d* takes on a hairline crack as I say it.

The silence settles on us again. And it suddenly strikes me how silly this all is. So he might crash in a car tomorrow? Heck, he can do that any day of the week, statistically speaking. He's got a shadowy figure in his past possibly out to get him? Well, I've done a tour in Afghanistan. I was trained to handle dangerous situations.

Running from a threat isn't what I trained for.

"Maybe we could… Maybe we're being too rash." The hope in my tone is so sharp it stings as I speak. "This is something—"

"Are you falling for me?" His tone is cold, too cold. He's never been like this before. "Because if you are, that means

I'm a piece of shit. Wasn't that the entire point of this exercise? Didn't you learn anything?"

He's doing it on purpose, pushing me away. Shoving me out of the path of danger. But it still bruises and batters me.

Headlights come from the opposite direction, flashing through the cabin as they come into the curve we're in. For a moment the other car dances close to the centerline, but my brain recognizes it as minor, nothing to worry about. The driver isn't about to sideswipe us.

"Oh, I learned." My own tone is cold, exactly how I used to talk to him. "I won't—"

The car swerves so suddenly I'm slammed against the door before the seat belt can catch me. My head is knocked so hard against the frame stars bloom in my vision like tracer rounds. I lose the thread of everything for a heartbeat, maybe two.

"*Fuck.*" That comes from Cassian as a half curse, half war cry. He's fighting with the steering wheel, trying to turn the car into the skid.

Except the car's not skidding. It's accelerating. Straight into the sheer drop-off to our right.

I grab the doorframe, the metal slick under my sweating palm. My foot stomps mindlessly on the floor, as if I might find a phantom brake there to stop us. My foot keeps finding nothing and we keep speeding up and up.

Cassian's foot is on the brake though, so hard he's lifting himself out of his seat. My pulse thrums as hard as the one in his neck, the both of us fighting—him against the car, me against my panic.

The screen in the console is blanked out, flashing static every other second. The car should be letting Cassian take over everything at this point, or at least shutting everything down.

Instead, it's trying to kill us.

Cassian's jerking the wheel this way and that, the tendons

in his hands standing out in stark relief. The wheel is barely moving and he's fighting as hard as he can.

"Jump clear," he grits out.

"No." Even if I could, I'd never leave him behind.

"You have—"

The car catches air, the road disappearing as the front end lifts. My stomach catches on gravity, leaves me behind with a sickening lurch.

Metal screams. The view out the windshield shifts, turns, until the road is where the sky should be.

My heart is going too fast. I can't make it stop.

Gravity seizes us again, pulls us down hard. Metal crunches. Glass shatters.

A spray of cold needles peppers my face. Something pops wetly in my shoulder as the seat belt slams into me, the roof racing for my head.

And then nothing.

CHAPTER 22

I tear at the seat belt that's trapping me, that's keeping me from Victoria. It doesn't budge—the fucking latch is busted and the catch has engaged, so I can't even squirm out from under it.

She's suspended upside down by her seat belt, blood running down her face and into her hair. Her eyes are half-closed and she's not answering me.

My fucking heart just dies at the sight. Up and stops running, leaving me an empty, scrabbling shell trying to get to her.

Fuck this seat belt. I reach over to the glove box, which was busted open in the crash, and pull out the knife I keep there. Two slashes later, I'm falling into the roof of the car.

Victoria's eyelids flutter and she makes a small moan.

"Stay with me, baby." I reach over and touch her cheek, her blood smearing over my fingertips. "I'll get you out of here."

She needs a doctor. Now. But first I have to get us out of this death trap.

My door is open a crack, the door latch bent and twisted by the force of the crash. I set my feet against it and push.

It doesn't move.

With a twist, I take in Victoria's window. Her door is still closed, but the window has shattered, several long wicked panes still in the frame. I can kick them out, but if I miss one and it catches her, she'll bleed. Bad.

It has to be my door then.

I set both feet against it, draw my legs in tight to my chest, and kick out with everything I have. One, two, three kicks like that and the door finally fucking gives.

"Cassian?" Victoria's voice is slurred, like she's fighting to keep awake. "I don't…"

"You don't have to do anything except stay with me." I push the door out another inch and try not to think about brain injuries and lasting effects and what it would mean if I lost her like this. I can't afford to have the black hole of that swallow me, not when she still needs me. "I've got it all under control."

I kick the door open another inch.

"Cassian?" This time her voice is stronger, the steel of her training entering it. Thank God she's my little soldier. "I can't get out on my own. I think my shoulder's dislocated."

Like she's giving a commanding officer a status report. I close my eyes for half a moment—God, the pain she must be in. And all because of me.

Because it is all because of me. This car was programmed to kill me, same as the other car was programmed to kill Ira.

I open my eyes. The guilt can come later, once she's safe.

"I'll get you out," I say. "Don't worry."

"I wasn't. I won't."

Those little words are like a shotgun blast to my heart. I kick even harder, pushing the door open two inches, now five, now ten. Now fully open.

I roll over to get her. The sight of her hanging there, blood streaming over her, is like a cold electric shock.

"I'm going to release the belt and catch you. It's your right shoulder that's hurt?"

She cranes her head, peering through the veil of her hair, and nods.

"This might hurt." I position myself, ready to catch her. "I'm so, so sorry if it does."

She laughs, of all things. "I'm already hurting. You can't hurt me more."

No, I'm not going to let that shatter me. Instead, I release her seat belt, catch her as she crumples into my arms. The living warmth of her is the best sensation I've felt ever.

She gives a raspy, serrated gasp. "Okay, that did…" She closes her eyes, breathing through her nose. "I'm okay now."

She's not, which is why I drag us both out as quickly as I can.

As I pull her free of the cabin, careful of her arm, I'm aware of a high, whistling whine. Like an animal desperate to reach trapped prey. That's when I realize the wheels are still spinning, driving as fast as they can.

With Victoria on one arm, I take in the underbelly of the car. The rear wheels are turning like a demon's inside them, racing to nowhere. And the front wheels are cranked as hard as they can be to the right, still trying to send the car off the road.

"Why is it still going?" Victoria asks.

I don't answer, because she doesn't need the burden of knowing that this accident wasn't an accident at all. I pull out my phone, dial Gage on his most private line. The one he answers at any hour.

"What happened?" he says as soon as he answers. "And who do I need to send?"

"Medic." I look down at Victoria, who's slumped hard against me. "Doctor too, one with emergency medicine training. And fast. Shit, just get me a mobile hospital as fast as you can."

"You?"

Shit, I wish it was. "Victoria."

"Fuck," Gage mutters. "I've got just the thing. Watch for a chopper coming. What else needs cleaning up?"

I take in the car, the engine still revving into the red. If Gage has any priests on staff, they'd be handy for an exorcism. He probably does.

"A tow truck," I say. "My car decided we needed to go off the side rail near Twin Peaks. Just like Ira's car did."

"What the fuck were you testing it for on your own?" Gage snarls. "Wait—*your* car? The Inspiron?"

"Yep," I bite out.

Gage realizes the implications immediately. "Shit. Okay, I've got an entire cleanup team coming your way. Still no cops, yeah?"

"No cops, thank God. And no witnesses."

The last thing we need is anyone else poking around in this. How to explain that the car was programmed to kill me? I can't. Shit, it would have been better if I'd been drunk.

"Good, keep it that way. I'll tell the rest of them and be with you in a few. Watch for the chopper."

He hangs up without another word.

I tuck Victoria closer to me, wishing there was someplace safe to let her lie down. But the side of the road is all sharp gravel and then the drop-off and the car... Yeah, we're not going anywhere near that car again.

"They're on their way," I tell her. "Listen for a helicopter. We'll get you out of here and into a doctor's hands."

She starts to shiver, her teeth chattering. But she's wrapped in a jacket and held tight to me, so she can't be cold. Which means shock is setting in.

"A medivac?" she asks weakly. "How much is that?"

As if the cost matters. As if anything matters but getting her to safety.

"Ever flown in a helicopter before?" I ask to distract her.

Every second that they're not here is like a hammer to my chest, but I can't let her see that.

She makes a noise that might have been a laugh if she was stronger. "I was in the Army. Of course I have."

A noise catches my ears, faint but coming closer. Something like an engine. And there's nowhere for us to hide because my car is on the side of the road, overturned, like some massive, dead cockroach.

A car appears from the direction we were coming, slowing as it approaches. It pulls over, and a man, wide-eyed and carrying his phone, gets out.

"You okay?" he yells to us. "I already called 911. The police and ambulance are on the way."

Fuck. Of course some Good Samaritan would show up and do the right thing. "Thanks," I grit out. "We're all right."

"Your wife"—he raises an uncertain finger toward Victoria—"she doesn't look good."

No, she looks like hell with blood running down her face, her arm cradled to her, and her skin a pale, sickly green. But she's upright, solely due to the force of her will.

"It's okay," she gets out, her voice still weak. She must hate that.

I have nowhere to shelter her from everyone seeing her though. A woman gets out of the car, followed by several teenagers, a boy and two girls. They immediately start filming with their cell phones.

"Oh shit," the boy says, "this is a serious wreck."

Great. This is going on the internet in seconds, I can already tell. From down the road, blue and red lights flash, a wailing siren catching up to them.

One of the girls elbows the other, whispering in her ear as she stares straight at me. I'm suddenly aware of the glass shards in my hair, the sticky swipe of something on my cheek—probably blood—and the tear in my shirtsleeve. I must look like absolute hell.

"Cassian?" Victoria's head lolls, and I just manage to keep her from falling over. "Is the chopper here?"

It isn't, but an ambulance is screaming toward us, accompanied by two police cruisers.

Before I can tell her that, her eyes roll back in her head and she completely passes out.

CHAPTER 23

Turns out that waking up from sedation doesn't get easier the more you do it.

This would be time number three for me, and it sucks just as bad as the first time. My throat is dry and burning, my mind is spitting out thoughts I know are nonsense, and my entire body thrums with dulled pain.

"I hate this." I make my mouth form the words.

"I know." Tess pats my hand, the one without an IV stuck in it. "But this was the last one. Your liver's all fixed now!"

My liver is *not* all fixed now. It has to regrow about a quarter of itself since my seat belt managed to slice into part of it. I had to go into surgery the moment I came into the hospital to figure out what was going on inside me, another operation to stitch up some more of my liver, and this one to cut away some dead tissue. The doctor promised me this was the last one.

"Good," I say with less enthusiasm than Tess. "I'm sick of doing this."

Tess's smile dims. "I know. I know how awful this has been. But they told me you could go home in a few days. And Cassian—" Her smile turns into a grimace.

I sit up, or try to. My incision screams. "He came? Again?"

I haven't seen Cassian since the accident, more than a week ago. I remember the ambulance coming—and that he promised me a helicopter ride—and then nothing until I woke up in the emergency room to a doctor telling me I had to go under again for surgery. Cassian might have been there—it was all very chaotic and dreamlike—but I haven't seen him since.

Tess looks like she'd rather cut her tongue out than talk. "He came once you were under. And stayed until you went into the recovery room. He's going to arrange for round-the-clock care for you."

I shift, the IV pulling at the insertion point at the back of my hand. "Did you talk to him?"

Meaning did she convince him that he's being an idiot? Cassian did that with my other surgery too—arrived right as I was going under, then left once I was out of anesthesia. It's like he wants to be close in case I die but can't bring himself to actually see me.

"I did." Tess's shoulders slump. "He thinks he's protecting you. If you saw how he looks…" Her expression is haunted. "It's bad. Gideon says he's never seen him like this."

"I wouldn't know, because I can't see him at all." My voice is so sharp one of the nurses glances over at me.

Tess looks at the nurse, then back at me. She lowers her voice. "There are some other issues too."

"Beyond a self-driving car trying to kill us?" I pitch my voice low too, because that particular detail doesn't need to be widely known. "What's happening with that? Have he and Morgan gotten closer?"

Tess shakes her head. "I don't know. They haven't told me much beyond that Cassian and Morgan are working on it. Probably because they know I'll pass whatever I hear on to you, and you're supposed to be healing. Not worrying."

It makes sense, but I still hate it.

"I deserve to at least see him." A thin film of desperation clings to the words.

"I agree," Tess says. "But Cassian doesn't. He said…" Her mouth twists and she gives a little sniff. "He said he's hurt you enough. That he wouldn't be like the other guys you've dated. That it's over and done, but he'll never forget you. That you were the one teaching him all the lessons."

My eyes sting and I blink away the burn. It sounds so final. So resolved. "If I can just talk to him, I can tell him that's silly. He hasn't hurt me."

Before she can stop herself, Tess glances down at my torso, at the spot where I've been cut open. Again. She takes a deep breath. "Remember when you told me Gideon was dangerous and that I should get away from him? I'm not going to say the same thing about Cassian, but this… this is bad." Her face goes very white. "When I got the call and then when I saw you here…"

I take her hand and squeeze. "I'm okay. And maybe you're right. Me charging in like I can fix things, like I have a duty to… Maybe I'm just being an asshole. Certainly I was never able to help you."

Tess shakes her head. "You could never be an asshole. And you've helped me by being my friend."

Okay, the tears are back now. "Well, I wanted to do more. I should have done more."

"You did everything you could, and it was more than enough." Tess wipes her eyes with her free hand. "Cassian told me one last thing to tell you too. He said, 'This is the only noble, unselfish thing I've ever done. Tell her to let me have this.'"

I thought I was boneless before, coming out of anesthesia and regaining control of my limbs, but those words flatten me. "Oh God," I whisper.

He's right. He is doing something he thinks is beautiful

here, giving me up for my own good. But he's wrong about one thing—it's not the only noble thing he's ever done.

But I won't be able to tell him that, because I'm going to honor his wishes.

"Yeah," Tess says slowly. "There wasn't much more arguing I could do after that."

"Me either." I stare at the wall, painted what I suppose is a soothing shade of lavender. This entire place is more like a high-end day spa than a hospital. I've noticed Wolfe Medical on several of the signs—I'm guessing Gideon paid a pretty penny for this corner of the hospital to be set aside for whoever he wanted to send through it. Or whoever was willing to pay a premium for the luxury package.

Luxury surgery. I almost laugh, which is weird, because my heart is cracked. Can they fix that here? Probably not.

I sigh, turn my head into the pillow. I've just woken up, but now I want to go right back to sleep. Preferably forever. Or at least until Cassian can come wake me up with a kiss. Which isn't going to happen.

Tess tugs at our linked hands, the gesture both affectionate and a warning. "There's more I haven't brought up. An added… wrinkle."

"What could be more wrinkled than this?" I point to my incision.

"It's lucky that you don't have your phone though," she says cheerily. "It could be worse if you were watching."

My face goes cold. "Watching what?"

"Do you remember the people who stopped for you guys? The kids with them?"

I vaguely do. Mostly I remember the ambulance. Or at least the lights. Everything else was a dark blur. Except for Cassian. He's very real and solid in my memories.

"I guess. Why?"

"They, uh, took a video. And posted it."

Of course they did. Because why let a perfectly good car

crash go to waste when you can share it with the entire world? "Okay, so some people have seen me looking awful." I don't like the idea, but I'll survive.

"There's more." Tess's expression tips further into pity. "They recognized Cassian. And the media picked it up, because a billionaire tech titan crashing his car with a beautiful woman with him? That's a meaty story. And the video helped it go viral. Super viral."

I swallow hard. "*Super* viral?"

Tess grimaces. "Yeah, that's the only way to describe it. Apparently there's some internet forum that follows Cassian's every move—like a cross between a fan site and a troll den—and they found out everything about you. Like… everything. They even posted your high school transcripts."

"Who would ever give a crap about my high school transcripts?" I'm trying to imagine what classes I even took in high school—ceramics? I think I also took a theater class?

Tess gives herself a shake. "The transcripts aren't the important part. I'm just trying to give you a sense of how deep they went."

"Trust me, I feel completely excavated now." My transcripts. Of all the… What kind of psychos would dig those up?

"It gets worse." Tess takes a breath, preparing herself.

Suddenly I already know. I can see exactly what they went for, how best to hurt me. "The kids," I whisper.

Tess nods. "They found your Instagram. And about the program. And then they found the kids' Instagrams and social media accounts. You were in some of their pictures. The media didn't ID the kids directly, but they did mention the program and…" Tess takes a shuddering breath. "It's kind of a clusterfuck."

I can tell by her face that it's more than that. "Give me my phone." I hold out my hand. "Please."

Tess, to her credit, only hesitates a moment before

reaching into her purse for it. "I already deleted your Instagram account," she says. "You wouldn't have wanted to read the comments."

My stomach drops. I force myself to unlock the phone.

My email program lists an ungodly number of unread messages. The number in the little red circle is so big I almost laugh. No one can have that many messages ever. It would take me days just to delete all of them.

I ignore my inbox and bring up my voice mail. There are fewer messages marked in red there, but still too many. And all from numbers I don't recognize. Great, so my phone number is out there somewhere too. I'll have to nuke my email account and my phone number.

Still, I don't care too much. I find the number I do recognize, queue up the message.

The voice of the head of the foster agency comes out of the speaker. She's apologetic, a touch confused. *Hey, Victoria. I hope... I hope you're okay. We saw the video and...*

There's a scrubbing sound like she's rubbing her eyes.

We've been getting a lot of calls. And emails. And attention. The state... they've gotten involved. I know it's not your fault, but this is a huge situation now.

A pause, so dark and deep my heart tumbles into it.

Well, we have to shut down your program. The director is all firm resolve now, the sympathy gone. *You understand why. People have been contacting the kids even. It's out of control and we have to shut it down for the kids' safety. You understand.*

There's no more message—she hangs up after that.

And I do. The kids have to be protected. I was asleep for all this and couldn't stop it. Couldn't even head it off. And that kills me.

What also kills me is that once again, I couldn't do what I was supposed to. Tess got hurt before, and the kids got hurt this time. Before, I lost my career. And now I've lost...

I take in a deep, shuddering breath. The program was

the one thing I did that felt meaningful. A duty I was pleased to perform. And even that's been torn away from me.

I want to cry, to collapse, to scream. But that wouldn't be befitting.

Instead, I square my shoulders, bring up a new text message. *I understand. Thank you for the opportunity.* I send that off to the director—I doubt she'd take any of my calls now. And even if she did, I wouldn't put her or me through the agony of it.

It's done. It's gone.

I hand my phone back to Tess. "Could you get rid of that?" I ask. "Wipe and then… I don't know." I'm tempted to tell her to burn it. But that wouldn't be responsible. "Recycle it, I guess."

Tess takes it, and it disappears into her purse. When her hand comes back out, she's holding a different, new phone. "They figured you'd need this. New number, new email, all of it. And…" She sets the phone in my palm with a troubled expression. "Cassian doesn't have this number. He specifically asked that he not know it."

Of course. He's cutting himself off from temptation.

My fingers curl around the phone. "He still knows where I live."

Tess bites her lip. "Actually, we're going somewhere else for your rehab. And Gage thinks that you probably should move."

So everything is going. I shut my eyes briefly. "Let me guess—Cassian's paying for it. All of it. And my job? Is that gone too?"

Tess looks so hurt I almost wish I hadn't been so bitter. "Harold can finish up this last job. We don't have anything coming up, so I'm closing the office until you're better." Her smile is tremulous. "I mean, it's kind of a dream, right, to have the time and money to take as long as you want to recover? And I'll be there to help. We can bring back Shield Solutions once you're one hundred percent again."

She's right. I should be recovering and not worrying about anything. Cassian has set it all up so beautifully that I can.

"Besides," she says, "lying low is probably for the best. There's media camped outside the hospital even. You being photographed will only stir it up again."

I wonder if Cassian told her that. If he's already got a plan to get his branding back under control, polished to the high shine he prefers.

I wonder if Jacinda is upset that the program ended so abruptly. I wonder if she's mad at me about it—she should be.

The nurse comes in then, taking the phone from me and setting it on my bedside tray. "Let's take your vitals," he says in a firm, reassuring voice. "Little spike in your blood pressure there."

I bet it was more than a spike, considering what Tess told me.

"That was my fault," Tess says apologetically.

"No, it's okay," I say quickly. "I reacted to something but… it won't happen again."

It can't, because there's nothing left to surprise me now that Cassian is out of my life.

CHAPTER 24

Morgan is still pissed at me.

I can see it in the way she moves around—short, sharp, like she's just holding back from hitting me. Morgan's always been wound a little tight, but this is beyond that. This is deeply pissed Morgan, not impatient to get on with things Morgan.

"Hand me that connector?" she asks, flicking her hand in the general direction without looking up.

"You need this one." I hand her a different one, the correct one.

She glares at it. "I'm pretty sure—"

"Victoria already tried it. It's this one."

Her name coming out of my mouth feels sharp, like it's going to slice my tongue open. Or maybe my heart, but that's already bleeding.

Morgan takes the connector from me, not touching my hand. "How did the surgery go?"

"Fine. The doctor said everything went better than expected. She's going home today."

"Did you see her?"

I nod. "She's looking better."

Morgan's frown deepens. "But you didn't talk to her

because she was under. You know, I'm pretty sure it's a HIPAA violation for the doctor to be telling you all this behind her back."

Probably. Whoever's in charge of HIPAA is welcome to try to take me to court. "When you're paying for it, it turns out the finer points of the privacy law don't matter."

Morgan snorts. "Typical."

Something about the way she says it puts me on edge, and I can't shake it off. Usually I can shake anything off and I do.

Usually I don't give a damn about much. Morgan's grumpy? Must be a day that ends in *Y*. I've said goodbye to a woman? Yet another day that ends in *Y*. I'm acting like a carefree, nihilistic bastard? Again…

Something about the wreck is making everything stick to me though.

"What the fuck does that mean?" I tilt my head, put on a challenging smile.

Morgan looks surprised for a moment, then her expression hardens. "Don't take this out on me. I just meant that normally nothing matters to you. You talk your way out of— or into—anything you want."

I've talked my way out of Victoria's life. Tess made that clear when she came back from the hospital the other day. She passed on my message about giving Victoria up and it being the only good thing I've ever done… and it was received loud and clear.

Morgan jams the connector into the slot with more force than necessary. "So don't get salty. It's just what you do."

"I'm never salty," I mutter. That's part of not giving a damn—salt is for people who care.

Morgan starts up her testing window, rubbing her face as she waits for it to load. "The update I pushed seems to be working," she says. "The security hole is patched now."

Meaning that no one can insert fatal instructions to the Inspiron through the flaw she discovered. When I told her that the car she helped designed tried to kill Victoria and me, she went bloodless. And then she worked round the clock to ensure it couldn't happen again.

We found the gap in the security where our enemy must have inserted the override program. Now we're hunting down the override itself, comparing the code in the Inspiron system to the one we originally built years ago.

I'm beginning to see how this killer thinks. They're smart, but not *that* smart. And I'm guessing they used the same program to kill Ira that they tried to use on me.

If it's true… My heart is heavy. The details are starting to form into a profile, a profile that only fits one person. The one person I don't want it to be.

But it's not entirely clear yet. And I'm still hoping it won't be whom I suspect.

"Good." I glance at Morgan. "That was fast."

Her smile is faint and bitter. "Yeah, well, it was kind of a big breach. Axel was furious when I told him."

"With you?" I ask sharply.

She turns her head slowly to stare at me. "No, not with me. You guys just won't give him a chance, will you? Look, I know he's not Tynan…" She quickly looks away, her jaw tightening.

That's not my problem with Axel—he's a superficial idiot is my concern—but I always thought that would be *Morgan's* problem with him.

I gentle my tone. "Things are very… chaotic what with Tynan possibly being alive. And this"—I gesture to the metal computer cases sitting on the workbench—"and this fucking mess. I want to make sure you aren't getting any more stress than you need. And I know I'm a massive contributor to the pile of shit that's getting dumped on you, and I'm sorry."

She narrows her eyes. "You're being sincere." She makes it sound like a crime. "You never used to be like this."

I can't help it—I start to laugh. "Jesus, and you're angry about that?"

Her expression clears, a faint smile tugging at her lips, and for a moment she's close to the old Morgan, the one before Ira died. "Not angry. It's surprising. A good surprise, I guess." She nods to the machines sitting before us. "I just wasn't expecting that in the middle of this shit storm." Her eyes are open, questioning when she looks back at me. "Is there any chance that you and she could…?"

My face goes cold and stiff. "No." I can only see Victoria lying in the hospital bed, pale and unconscious, internally bleeding because she got too close to me. "And I think you understand why."

Morgan dips her head and turns back to the computer. Her chin is trembling as she begins to type in commands. On the screen, line after line scrolls by as our search program looks for the code the killer snuck in there.

"I'm still mad at you," Morgan says. "I mean, after what happened with your car, it's probably not your fault what happened to Dad… but I'm still angry." She types with sharp, percussive precision and doesn't look at me.

"You have every right to be."

"Raven wants to forgive all of you." Her fingers don't slow on the keyboard. "Or at least start to pretend that things are okay again. She wants everyone at her place—Dad's place— for Gage's unbirthday in two days."

I take in her stance, how she absolutely won't look at me. But as she curves herself over the keyboard, her hip is cocked toward me. Just the barest amount. The tiniest opening.

She's not ready to entirely stop being mad. But she wants to start stopping being mad. If I give her a push, she'll take that path. If I don't…

"I suppose we could make it," I say neutrally. "Gage is looking forward to it."

Her spine softens a fraction. "He's not. But Raven would be disappointed if he didn't get his party."

"None of us wants to disappoint her."

Morgan releases a breath like she's accomplished something difficult. "Good. I'm glad it's settled." She frowns, leans closer to the screen. "Oh shit. What's that?"

I read through the lines of code. Immediately my brain recognizes what the complex abbreviations and commands are saying—because I wrote it.

This is the bit of code telling the car what to do when humans behave like… humans. Specifically when humans get a little wonky while driving through a curve. Exactly like I was doing last night. And probably exactly like Ira was doing when he died.

"Here." I point to a series of lines I didn't write. "When the car is coming into a curve, if another car is coming the opposite way, there's room for… wobble."

Morgan's gaze goes unfocused as she pictures it. "Wobble for you? Or the other car?"

"Other car. It's instinctive, especially going into a curve, especially at night, to drift into the other lane. But the system has to know, is it just people not thinking? Or is it a maneuver the car needs to respond to?"

Morgan nods slowly. "Does it learn from each instance too?"

"Of course. But here, this isn't learning. It's telling the car if it's in that situation and there's some wobble from the other driver that it needs to swerve. And swerve hard."

Basically, it's telling the car to run off the road. And the code is also disengaging the driver override if this situation occurs. To an onlooker, it would make it seem like the driver is overreacting to the lane drift from the other car. It's not elegant, but it would work.

It almost did.

"He used the exact same code in the Inspiron," Morgan

says. "Or she did. Do you think it was the same person who broke into Gideon's house?"

I shake my head. "No, this seems... too blunt for them. Whoever put the code in our system panicked when they learned it was sent to me, so they tried the same thing in my car. This isn't well thought out. But it was almost effective enough."

"Hang on." Morgan holds up a finger, then opens a new command window. "I need to see if this code was pushed to all Inspiron cars or just yours. It might narrow down our suspects."

The way she says *our* catches at me. It reminds me of how Victoria threw herself into this, made us a team. God, I miss her. Not that Morgan isn't smart, not that she isn't the perfect person to hunt down this code... but she's not Victoria.

No one else will ever be.

"Don't drive your Inspiron until we catch this guy," I say gruffly. "Or woman. Or whoever did it."

The name tingles on the tip of my tongue, but I don't say it. I can't poison that relationship if I'm not right. Morgan is already too far into this mess with us—the least I can do is warn her not to drive the car.

At least I was able to get Victoria clear of all this.

"I figured that out the moment I heard about the crash," she says. "Axel also told me not to. He got me a rental for the time being."

The fond affection in her voice makes my gut tighten. I could have that with Victoria if my life wasn't so fucked up.

"Good." I pull out my phone and start to check my latest messages, partly to keep myself busy while I wait for the search to finish and partly to stop thinking about Victoria.

The first message brings her screaming back. One of my PR people—Sandro—has sent me an article from some online news site with new revelations about Victoria and her past. Sandro wants to know if he can call in his contacts there to squash the story and any new ones coming down the line.

Do it, I write back. *Kill each and every story you see and the ones that haven't even been written yet.*

It's been like this since the crash, me and my entire team putting out flare-ups of media attention. The mainstream sites were mostly easy to cow, but the forums were tougher. I've had to buy out several hosting companies to shut those down, and there's still some I haven't been able to crush. Yet.

My Instagram has been silent since the crash. Surviving a deadly car crash fits exactly nowhere in my branding strategy, and since it's all people can think about at the moment, it's best to not release anything except something official and bland and forgettable from the company itself.

Victoria hopefully hasn't seen any of this. I told Tess specifically I would handle all of it, and Victoria was only to heal. Tess seemed to take it very seriously.

I've resisted asking Tess since. Because the temptation to ask for Victoria's new number at the same time is so strong I know I'll give in. I have to stay strong, for her safety.

"Aha." Morgan leans back from the computer. She waggles her fingers. "The code is nowhere in our servers or our system."

"You're sure?" This isn't something to be less than one hundred percent about.

She shrugs. "I mean, I'll do a deeper dive when I get into the office, but given that whoever did this used the exact same code as before, I'm guessing they wouldn't be great at hiding things. So…" She looks up at me. "It was only put on *your* car. Probably updated manually by someone with access to it."

I look away, hoping she can't read the expression on my face. This confirms my suspicions… but I don't want her to guess yet. Not until I can dig deeper.

"Well, that narrows it done some" is all I say. "And I'm glad it wasn't in your entire system."

Morgan studies me for a beat longer, then says, "Me too. And we found that security hole we needed to patch anyway." Her phone buzzes and she glances at it. "There's Axel, wondering where I am. I should go." She hesitates. "You're... you're okay? I mean, with the accident and..."

"I'm fine." I make my tone reassuring, my smile calm and distant. Just far enough away that she won't push harder. "I'll keep at this. For every answer we find, a million more questions sprout."

I think of the scrap of paper inside the self-driving system —I still can't connect it to my prime suspect. And of course there's still the question of why.

Why kill Ira?

I'm not going to ask his daughter that though. It's something I'll have to work through on my own. Fucking Tynan, dumping this into my lap.

"Thanks for all your help." I open the door for her. "I can take it from here. On my own."

CHAPTER 25

I have never been so bored in my life.

Or miserable. Or depressed. Or heartbroken.

Turns out that sitting and being waited on hand and foot is great for healing my body but not so much my heart and mind. I have nothing to do but obsess over how I have nothing to do. And that the man I'm half in love with has sworn to never see me again.

Okay, more than half in love with. Hours and hours with only my own thoughts has given me more than enough time and space to realize that.

The nurse comes in—Dee is her name—to check on me. "Quick blood pressure check," she says, as if it's the greatest treat in the world to be able to do that. I actually really like Dee—it's impossible to dislike someone who's so legitimately nice—but I also would like more wallowing time. It's hard to wallow when Dee is so darn happy.

I'm tempted to ask if this is really necessary as she straps the cuff on my arm, but I don't. It's her job, and my being a brat is only going to make it harder. We both know I don't give the orders here.

"How long do we need to keep checking it?" I ask instead.

Her glance at me is filled with sympathy. "I know this is

no fun. You're healing nicely. We just want to make sure you keep on this path."

We meaning the team of medical professionals Cassian has assembled to care for me, which includes three doctors, almost a dozen nurses, and two physical therapists. Now that my liver is regenerating, I can focus on my dislocated shoulder, which turns out to be way more painful and difficult than my internal injuries. But with all this care, I'm recovering much faster than I could have ever hoped.

When I'm done here, I'll be even stronger, healthier than I was before the crash. Which is probably the point. Cassian's working out his guilty conscience.

"Perfect," Dee announces as she types my numbers into her phone. Nobody does physical medical records anymore. "We'll check again before bed."

I give her a weak smile. "Thanks."

"Do you want me to turn on the TV or bring you a book or…?" She looks around at the lavish apartment we're in, with its view of the bay and Marin. "Or your knitting?"

It's not my knitting; it's Tess's. She thought maybe she could get me hooked on it. Which, knitting is fine and all, but I want to be *doing* something.

I grab my phone from the coffee table. "I'll just play on my phone for a while."

Dee gives the tiniest of sighs. Probably because she thinks the screen time is bad for me, and she'd be right. "Okay, but if you want anything else, let me know."

Once she's gone, I pull up all the social media sites I shouldn't be looking at. Thankfully, it seems that the story of our crash is less and less interesting with each passing day. Even the forums have gone mostly quiet except for a few diehards. The ones that put up pictures of my address are completely gone from the internet, scrubbed as if by magic. Or a very talented marketing firm with many, many lawyers backing them up.

I switch over to the email program, which is set up with my brand-new, supersecure email address. There isn't a single spam message or offer from some company or another for me to *buy, buy, buy, right now!*, just a quick note from someone at Cassian's company telling me that the effort to manage this crisis was continuing, but they expected things to be settled completely in a few days.

There's nothing from Cassian. I'm not expecting anything, but it's still a pinching shock each time I see he hasn't reached out.

"Hey," Tess calls out from the front door.

I quickly put my phone away and grab the knitting. Tess is very disapproving of my spending time on the phone—it's not therapeutic.

"Hey," I say, innocently purling when she comes in. "I didn't hear the door."

"Teddy let me in," she says. Teddy is another one of my nurses—one just isn't enough. Tess sets some take-out containers on the coffee table. "I brought you some scones from Arizmendi."

I grab for the bag. "That's the best news I've had all day."

Tess looks me over. "You look better, but vacation doesn't really suit you."

I swallow a bite of currant scone. "Any news on the apartment?" Now that my address has been plastered all over the internet, I need to find a new place to live. Someone at Cassian's company is working on finding me a temporary place, just like they're dealing with the rest of the fallout.

Tess shakes her head. "Cassian didn't like the one place they found. Said it wasn't you."

If she's trying to make me forget about him, that's not helping. "I could go look myself and say if it's me or not. Besides, what is *me?* A bed, a bathroom, a working stove— that's about all I need."

"Don't sell yourself short."

Slowly I lower the scone. I hate myself as I do it, but I have to ask, "Have you seen him?"

Tess goes still. "He looks awful. Like this is breaking him up inside."

I should be pleased he's suffering too, but I'm not. "I really want to get back to my life," I say quietly.

"I know." Tess is sympathetic but bracing. "And you will, very soon. You've been through a lot. Take some time."

I ponder that for a second. While I'm sitting here, not doing anything, the world just keeps on going. Cassian keeps searching for whoever did this, Tess keeps on with Shield Solutions, the dogs at the shelter still need homes, my foster kids get on with their lives.

What makes me think I can fix any of it? I've never been able to before. And yet…

"I don't want to take any more time," I announce. "I've already taken way too much time. Years, in fact."

Tess frowns. "I don't understand."

It's suddenly so clear; I have no idea why I didn't see it sooner. "Ever since I left the Army, I've just been spinning my wheels. With my job, with men, even with the foster kids. Taking small, easy things, not daring to do more. Afraid to do more."

"You've never been afraid of anything," Tess says hotly.

"But I have been, of everything, and I was too much of a coward to show it." I stand up, my shoulder twinging and my incision snapping. I welcome the pain because it reminds me I'm still alive. I can still fight. "I'm going to remake the foster program into something bigger and better. But I'm going to need donors for it. And to convince the animal shelter and the foster agency to start it up again."

Tess blinks up at me. "I like where this is going."

I nod because I do too. I feel powerful in a way I haven't in a long time. Like I've got my rudder reattached and can go zooming forward instead of in circles. "I'm going to need a marketing agency for this. A really good one."

Tess sucks in a sharp breath. "Are you sure about this? Really, really sure?"

I take a moment, probe my heart. "Yeah. This is the right thing to do. Even though I'm scared. Even though I might fail... again. But I have to do it."

Tess's smile is wide and bright. And a touch conspiratorial. "I know where you can find him tonight."

My eyes widen. I can see Cassian again in just a few hours. And hopefully show him how stupid he's being. "Where?"

Tess leans in. "I'll tell you all about it. And we'll make your battle plan."

A battle plan. Exactly what I've been needing. "Let's get to it."

CHAPTER 26

It's never been so hard to act like I don't give a fuck. I've been in this situation countless times before—all of us collected together, celebrating someone's unbirthday, acting as if we're one big happy family.

This time though, Oscar, Morgan, and Raven aren't oblivious about what the rest of us have done. And I know that the guilt we share for Ira's death… shouldn't be so equally parceled out. One of us is more responsible than all the rest.

I'm here to mend relations with Morgan and Raven and to figure out if my suspect really is guilty. It's why Tynan sent me the system—I'm the man who can see beneath the surface to what people really want, the things they can't even confess to themselves.

I need to figure out why they'd want Ira dead. Why they'd need me dead.

My stomach is filled with lead, and I haven't even cornered my quarry yet. This is going to be more difficult than I ever imagined.

I find myself wishing for Victoria, for her easy, determined strength. She's so goddamned clear-eyed—she wouldn't hesitate over this for a moment. I could use some of that clarity.

Instead, it's just going to be me and my fucked-up moral compass.

Archer comes up to me—I'm alone in a corner, nursing a drink.

"Any progress on that code?" His voice is pitched low, which I'm grateful for. I don't want my quarry to get suspicious just yet.

I shake my head. "Not from the last time we talked. Morgan went through the Inspiron servers with a fine-tooth comb—the code isn't there. So now we're going through my security logs, seeing who had access to my car over the past few weeks."

"Is that a lot so far?"

I take a drink, looking over the room. "A fair amount." But really, there was only one name I looked for. A name I already knew I was going to find.

The pattern keeps coming back to one person. Motive and opportunity for both crashes.

"What about the notebooks?" I've managed to put together a thin motive, but it's more of a gut feeling at this point than anything sturdy. I need more if I'm going to move against my suspect. And I'm pretty sure the rest of this puzzle lies in the notebooks.

Archer releases a tight sigh. "I've managed to decode them into something like English. But while I can get everything to assemble into recognizable words, it's all gibberish. The words aren't arranged into anything structured. It's all random."

"Shit," I mutter. "A second layer of encryption."

Ira was a careful guy but never paranoid. Not like that. Which means...

"He knew something was going to happen," I say. "Something that he couldn't stop. Whatever is in those notebooks is what he died for." I glance around the room. No one's paying attention to us. "We can't discuss this here."

Archer follows my gaze. "So you're like Gideon—you think it was one of us."

Oh, now that's a loaded statement. It's someone in this room, but not one of *us* like Archer is saying. But I don't know if he's ready to hear that. I don't know if I'm ready to say it.

"I just want to be careful," I say. "I haven't discussed this with anyone yet, and the girls…"

I let Archer fill that in with whatever he wants.

Oscar comes over then, a glass of wine in his hand. His face is flushed—that must be far from his first glass. He doesn't usually overindulge. His smile is too wide, his eyes bright but unfocused.

"What are you two conspiring about over here?" He drops his voice to a mock whisper.

Archer can't quite get his smile to look real. "Business. Cassian is always pushing me to do more marketing. Personally, I think he just wants a new pool and is trying to get me to pay for it."

I already have two pools, one indoor and one outdoor, which in San Francisco is the height of aquatic overkill. "What I really need is a steam room." I wink at Oscar. "To keep me warm when the fog rolls in."

Oscar laughs and slaps me on the back. "Exactly." His hand clasps my shoulder.

Archer's attention is already lost. "I need to go talk to Gage," he mutters, mostly to himself. "See you."

Oscar doesn't even glance at him. His grip remains tight on my shoulder. "How are you feeling?" His concern is so intense it's like a physical force. "You really should have let the paramedics look you over. And a therapist—"

"I've been through worse," I say quickly.

Oscar's face falls. "Right. We all have." The way his voice dips toward grief… "But you should still take it easy. You know, maybe you're under too much stress. Maybe that's why this happened."

This is exactly like Oscar—to offer me comfort, to tell me I deserve good things too. That I should take some time off, that I was too stressed. So stressed that I wrecked a car.

"Maybe," I say, as if I don't care that Victoria could have died. As if it doesn't feel like my heart is missing from my chest without her here. "But I didn't get to where I am by taking it slow."

"Of course not," Oscar says. "How is the young lady?" He asks so casually it's almost as if he doesn't know what Victoria means to me. Maybe he doesn't.

"Recovering." I finish off my drink with a quick flick of my wrist. "She's going to be completely fine."

I've been on the phone daily with her doctors, sometimes hourly. And of course Tess keeps me updated too.

"Good." Oscar nods his head like he's glad that's settled. "All the business with the media stories—man, those tabloids are awful. I hope you didn't see any of that."

There's the perfect mix of outrage and concern there. Nothing to be suspicious about.

"My team is working on it. Things are already quieting down." I take a moment to study him, wondering how to press this next thrust. "What have you been up to?"

He gives a self-deprecating shrug. "I was thinking about what you said. About retiring. And I'm not ready. With everything that Ira and I left undone… It's time to take that up again, get that project going."

Prickles run up my neck. "The neuronal-interface thing?" I don't look at him as I ask.

I'm being too offhand—that project had the potential to revolutionize… everything. A computer chip that can talk directly to the brain, read the neuronal code and take commands from it? It would be the most amazing science fiction come to life.

No one was surprised when that project fizzled out after Ira's death. Of course it was too ambitious to work.

Oscar nods. "We had such hopes for it. But after Ira was gone…" His gaze travels over to Morgan, who's talking with Axel.

"I thought you shut that project down." It's been five years—no way did he keep all those people on the payroll, doing nothing.

"It can be revived." His focus stays on Morgan. "And I think it would be perfect for Morgan. Reviving her father's legacy and all."

My prickles turn to needles. "But she's already working for Inspiron. She seems happy there."

"Self-driving cars are… pedestrian, compared to computer-brain interfaces." Oscar smiles at his own joke. "She's too smart to stay working on those forever. Besides, maybe we could get her away from Axel." He gives me a conspiratorial look. "You boys have never liked Axel."

He's right—we've never liked Axel. Either because we don't think anyone's worthy of Morgan, or because… because we still believe she should be with Tynan.

"I don't know that I'd interfere with Morgan's love life," I say lazily. "Might lose some fingers."

Oscar laughs, short and sharp. "We could probably convince her together."

The hell of it is, I kind of agree. Morgan is a genius, and she would make a huge mark, carrying on Ira's work. And yeah, I don't like Axel. And being pulled into this by Oscar, as if my opinion matters and he needs my help… it's tempting. He values me.

Before I can formulate a response, Victoria walks in.

It's like the sun coming out from behind a bank of storm clouds, and I swear I feel my heart blink against her brightness.

A low murmur runs through the room because everyone

knows that I've given her up, pushed her hard and far away to keep her safe. The guys all stare as if unsure what to do.

Tess is grinning, hiding her delight behind her hand. So this is something they planned.

Raven starts for Victoria, her arms open in welcome. "I'm so glad you came!" And she really is. "Can I get you—"

Victoria holds up a hand, all strict, straight-backed officer. "I came here for a reason."

Her gaze finds me across the room, pierces me. And then she says the sweetest thing I've ever heard. "I need you."

CHAPTER 27

"I need you."

Cassian's eyes go wide. Someone gasps.

Next to him, Oscar nudges Cassian. Cassian's expression shutters.

"For a marketing campaign," I say quickly. "You lost me the foster-kids project, so you owe me."

"Foster kids?" Raven's eyes go liquid with sentiment. "You're helping foster kids?"

"Was," I clarify. "The foster agency had to stop it with the storm of media and internet attention. It wasn't safe for the kids after I got doxed."

Cassian's jaw goes tight. "They didn't tell me the program got shut down. Only that your Instagram was deleted."

I lift my chin. "I didn't tell your PR people about it, so don't punish them. But I have a new concept. A bigger one. But I'll need your help to sell it. And like I said, you owe me."

His expression goes flat again. "Right. Because I can sell anyone anything. So that's why you came."

The tension in the room is thick, tight, like a power line ready to snap.

Raven clears her throat. "Maybe you two want to talk in Dad's office? It's quieter in there."

Quieter and more private she means.

"Could we?" I ask gratefully. With everyone staring at me, it's too hard to say what I really want to. And Cassian… he doesn't look happy at all to see me.

"Sure." Raven's smile is tentative. "It's this—"

"I remember where it is," Cassian says curtly, cutting in front of her.

"Son," Oscar says, half in concern, half in warning.

My heart does a sidestep, because Cassian is never short like this. Even when he's furious, he's not deliberately rude. Or sullen.

Maybe I'm too late. Maybe it was always too late.

But I follow him to the office, which is the perfect picture of a gentleman's study. Heavy mahogany furniture, seats covered in buttery leather, and a wet bar with cut-crystal decanters.

The moment the door closes, before I can even take a seat, Cassian rounds on me. He stalks so close I instinctively back up against a table. He doesn't stop, not until I can see the flecks of green deep in his brown eyes.

He takes hold of my arms, leans over me. My heart is doing a great impression of a jackhammer, although I'm not afraid.

"I'm well aware of what I owe you," he grits out. All the pretense of lazy indifference has been completely stripped away, leaving this rough emotion behind. "Do you think a moment goes by that I don't think about what I did to you? What it cost you to be associated with me?"

I swallow hard. "I don't… That's not what I meant."

He doesn't seem to hear me. "You want a man who can scam someone out of anything? Or everything? You want a fucking scoundrel? You've got him."

His mouth crashes into mine.

The kiss should be rough, fierce, given his mood, but

that's not Cassian's way, not ever. It's deep but tender, intense but intimate. It's perfect.

He breaks our connection, sets his forehead against mine. "You weren't supposed to come find me. I can't keep you away if you're this close."

"It was your dumb idea to keep me away. And I never thought you were a scammer or a scoundrel. At least not since I got to know you."

He releases an exhale that's too sad to be a sigh. "Don't do this. I'm trying so hard to be a better man and leave you alone. But I smell your soap in my sheets, the cats wander the house like they're looking for you…" He closes his eyes tight for a moment. "And I keep seeing you hurt, hanging from the seat belt with blood running down your face."

His tone has gone as colorless as a nightmare. I shudder because that haunts me too.

"It's not safe for you to be with me." The determination has come back into his eyes, but he doesn't let go of me.

I think of everything I can say—that the world is dangerous no matter what, that anything can happen anytime, that he's worth all the danger… but I know he's thinking about those car wheels still turning as fast as they could even when the car was upside down. About how someone tried to kill the both of us.

"You're right," I say slowly. "It's not safe for me to be with you." I lock my gaze to his. "Which is why I'm the perfect woman for you. I didn't join the Army to be safe. That's never sounded good to me. Which is probably why I kept going out with the wrong guys. I wanted bad, but… but I guess I was waiting for the right kind of bad. And you, Cassian? You're exactly my kind of bad."

A wild hope flares on his face before he ruthlessly squashes it. "And if I don't agree? If I don't want you in my life no matter what you want?"

For a moment my heart stops. Then I see the flicker deep

in his eyes. "Okay then," I say, lifting my chin challengingly, "convince me of that. Sell me on it. Should be easy for you, right?"

He closes his eyes in defeat. "Fuck," he mutters. "You know I can't."

"Why not?" My pulse is going double time.

His eyes snap open, the emotion there so raw I gasp. "Because I love you. And I'm a selfish enough shit to not let you go no matter how much danger I put you in."

I kiss him then, quick, light touches of my mouth over his forehead, cheeks, lips. My hands run over him before I settle my arms around his neck, curving myself into him.

"I love you too," I say, a sense of deep rightness coming over me.

He pulls me so hard into him I give a squeak. My ass hits the top of the table, my legs hanging off. "If you knew what those words do to me," he growls. "I can't show you here..." He glances around the office, grimacing. "It'd be like making love to you in my dad's room. And then there's everyone outside."

I raise an eyebrow. "A real bad boy would just do it."

He releases an exhale like a dragon breathing flame. "Then be a good girl and don't scream."

I lick my lips as he pushes my skirt up my thighs, already breathing heavily. I bite back a noise as he finds my folds, caresses my clit.

"You could kiss me to keep me quiet."

He laughs, low and rough. "And make it easy for you?" He pushes my panties aside, curls a finger so deep inside me I can't help my jagged moan. "No. Now remember to be good."

I can't though, not when he's playing my body, my rising pleasure, like an instrument only he knows how to play. A noise threads out of my throat, high, rising, and I can't hold it back any more than I can hold back my climax.

"Please," I beg, and I'm not sure what I'm asking for. More? Less? Mercy?

He puts his other hand to my cheek, his expression softening. "Ah, baby. When you ask me like that…"

In the next moment, his pants are unzipped and he's inside me, his thick cock taking the place of his fingers. I clench around him, the first ripples of an orgasm moving through me.

When I come, I do scream. But he's groaning too, almost as loud as I am, pouring his own climax into me.

I fall against him, limp and sweaty, my arms still around his neck. "Sorry," I murmur. "I screamed. Really loud."

A laugh rolls out of him. "They won't come investigate."

Heat creeps into my cheeks. "They won't have to—they already know what we did."

He lifts his head to give me a look. "What happened to Danger Girl?"

"Getting caught naked by your friends doesn't count as real danger." I wriggle down off the table and start to set myself to rights.

Cassian's expression goes stony as he zips up his pants. "No, but… I think I know who fucked with the car. Both of them."

I go very still, a chill creeping up my skin. "Who?" I ask in an almost whisper.

He only shakes his head.

"Is it someone… here?" This time I do ask in a whisper.

His mouth goes so flat it almost looks cruel. "If I'm wrong and say it here, to all of them… I'll break something that can never be repaired."

I reach for him, so solid and warm. For all that he pretends not to care, he cares so deeply it sometimes takes my breath away. "Didn't that thing already get broken when Ira died? When you almost died?"

"Maybe." He leans into my touch. "What I really need is

more evidence. If I'm going to throw this bomb, I need to be one hundred percent sure of the target."

"Take it from me," I say. "You can never be one hundred percent sure of the target."

He takes my hand, pulls me into his arms. "Let's go home." His breath ruffles my hair. "I've missed you and I want to tell you… everything."

I curl into him, savoring his closeness. "I've been waiting for you to say that."

CHAPTER 28

There's a certain peace in accepting I'm a selfish asshole. Especially if accepting that means I get to have Victoria too. Besides, she helps me to be a *better* selfish asshole.

We're back at my place, together in the workroom, going through everything Morgan and I uncovered in the car operating systems. She's sketched for me her initial ideas for a new project, one more ambitious than putting kids and dogs together. I give her some ideas for pitching it to the foster agency.

I haven't told her who my main suspect is, but I think she's starting to guess. She doesn't push me, just lets me keep giving her marketing ideas.

Bruiser is sprawled out—that cat has some serious sprawling skills—on our notes, using them for a bed. Or simply letting us know what he thinks of our silly human pursuits.

Bane is perched on a chair in a corner, not close enough to touch but close enough to let us know he's there. When he came in and let Victoria actually see him, I was stunned. I don't think even Lawford has ever gotten a good look at Bane.

I'm taking it as a sign: Victoria is meant to be here, with me.

"You should talk to Javi about getting together a pitch packet," I say. "He's a genius at that. And he knows the right people in the media. He should have been talking to you about…" I spin my finger in the air. "All the shit that's happened to us."

"He did, but…" Victoria shrugs. "I don't know, he has some weird email address that's all numbers and letters. It keeps bouncing into spam no matter what I do."

I reach for her laptop. "Let me…"

Numbers and letters. A meaningless string.

It's like the clouds in my brain have parted and I can see everything clearly for the first time. "It's a secure messaging address. Jesus, of all the…" I shake my head as I reach for my own laptop. He just can't make it easy.

"Yeah, I said it was." Victoria frowns as she looks up at me. "That's not what you're talking about."

"No." I call up the secure messaging app most of us in tech use. No one can trace this back to me or my company unless they're very, very good. I open a new message window. "He probably used this messaging system. Probably."

"Who did?"

I force myself to stop, slow down. "The paper we found in the self-driving system—it's an address. A random, generic address within a secure messaging app that can't be traced to anything. And is the only way to contact Tynan."

She sits back as she ponders that. "But the string was in the notebooks. Many times. That can't be an accident."

"It isn't. And I think the string still has some meaning we haven't cracked yet. But I'm betting that Tynan reused it for this."

"But if he didn't have the notebooks, then how would he know the string was meaningful?"

Huh. I chew on that for a moment. "Tynan was working

with Ira on some chip before he died. We were so busy with the self-driving system I didn't pay it much attention. But maybe the string is related to that project."

"Can we find that project again? Go through it?"

I nod. "It's something to do with neuronal interfaces. Getting computers to talk to nerve cells and vice versa. I'll bet it's all still there on Ira's old hard drives."

The cursor blinks at me inside the empty message box. First I need to see if this hunch is correct.

I got your package, I type. *And your message. C.*

Victoria bites her lip once I hit Send. "What if it isn't him? And you've just wrong numbered some rando?"

"Then that would be the perfect cap to this fucked-up mess." Somehow I don't think it's true though.

It doesn't take long to find out. The app pings and a reply pops up in the window.

Took you long enough. I see you already tested the system—you were lucky. That time.

It's definitely Tynan, because he's referring to my recent crash. And his long-ago one.

My pulse is going so fast it's running off with my breath. Tynan really is alive. I suppose I can ask for better proof of life, like a picture with today's newspaper, but this is enough.

"Is that him?" Victoria asks as she peers at the screen.

I nod. "Yeah. He heard about my accident. Our accident." I can't help my quick glance to her midsection where her liver is still healing. "He thinks it's because we were testing the old system."

She bites the corner of her lip. "Still, is there some old code word you can use? Something only he would know and not the others?"

I sift through my memories of Tynan—the first time meeting him, when we were all too sullen and up our own asses to care about anyone else. Tynan was not as into it as the rest of us were, but he was also somehow apart. Like the edge we were all affecting wasn't so interesting to him.

He also wore a hoodie with a local punk band on it, very niche. You only knew them if you lived in the Bay Area and you only got their merch if you went to one of their live shows.

It might be the perfect test.

How's that old hoodie of yours? I type. *Still have it?*

"Hoodie? Like a sweatshirt?" Victoria's confusion is adorable. I want to tweak her nose, and I am not a nose tweaker.

Love has really fucked up my playboy game.

"Yep." I sit back, wait for his reply. "He had a one-of-a-kind one. Something no one else had. Let's see if he gets my hint."

Victoria settles closer to me, pressing her lovely length against me. I reach over and snare her waist, holding her loosely. I'll have to type one-handed, but it's worth it.

A new message pops up: *The Deva Station one? Yeah. I was wearing it... when it happened.*

I catch my breath. Shit, I completely forgot that Tynan would have left everything behind when he disappeared. Which I should have remembered, because I had to help go through all his stuff. Gideon probably still has most of it, stuck in a storage locker somewhere. But this isn't the time for that.

"It's him," I say.

Victoria moves away so I can type, and I resist the urge to pull her back.

Once my fingers start moving, it all pours out of me: *I got the system to throw the error again. It's specific, meant to send the car off the road in very specific circumstances.*

Someone put the same bug in my own car, almost killing me. Morgan tracked down the identical code in our original system.

Whoever is doing this isn't very inventive. But the bug was effective.

I realized why you sent the system to me: you wanted me to root out who on the inside betrayed Ira. It took a while to figure out. And I'm not entirely certain I'm right.

I cycle through all the suspects in my head again, weighing and discarding the evidence. I even include Tynan and myself in the list.

But I keep coming back to the same answer. The one that hurts the most.

But here's my best guess as to who did it:

The cursor blinks over the empty space for what feels like an eternity.

I realize Victoria is watching me steadily, solemnly. Like she knows I can do this.

The fallout will be bad. But I can survive anything if I have her.

Oscar, I finally write.

Victoria's hand comes to my shoulder. I take it up, press a kiss to it.

"I know you didn't want it to be him," she says in almost a whisper.

"I didn't want it to be anyone," I say tonelessly. "But I especially didn't want it to be him."

My father had never really been a father—I was too much of a disappointment to him. Losing him didn't hurt. Ira… losing Ira was bound up with my own crushing guilt over his death.

Oscar was supposed to be the father I could love without hurting. Except he wasn't.

I keep Victoria's hand in mine, drawing on her steady strength.

"Why would he do it?"

"I don't know," I admit. "That's the next mystery to solve in this. But I'm guessing the answer is in the notebooks."

The typing bubble pops up in the message window—Tynan is responding. I wonder if he suspected Oscar ever. Or if he only suspected one of the guys. Or maybe even Raven or Morgan.

Probably not Morgan. And Raven was too kind to even hurt an insect. It's a cliché, but it's true in her case—I've seen her scoop up spiders to release outside, screaming quietly in horror the entire time.

The bubble stays up for a while, but in the end, the only word that comes through is *fuck.*

Indeed. That about sums it up.

Have you decoded your notebook? I ask.

No.

Although you can't read tone on the internet, I sense Tynan's irritated impatience.

Where are you? Where have you been? I'm typing furiously, tossing questions at him as quickly as my fingers will allow. I played his stupid game with the system; now he can tell me what the fuck is going on with him.

When are you coming back? Why didn't you come back? Who did you hire to steal the notebooks? Why didn't you come find us right after?

More comes to me, things that aren't questions. *We thought you were dead too, and it fucked us up. Especially Morgan. You should have been here; we could have figured this out together.*

But I hold back. That can all come when he finally comes back, which he has to do. And we can all do it together, because he left all of us hanging.

I wait for his reply.

Nothing. Not even a typing bubble. Then his icon, the generic one the program assigns to everyone, goes gray. He's logged off. He damn well saw my questions and decided not to answer them.

"Oh," Victoria says, offended. "He just left."

I push back from the desk with a sigh. "Yeah. Apparently that's his MO now."

Victoria watches me, her gaze open. I feel like I can do anything when she looks at me like that, like I'm worthy of that kind of attention.

"What now?" she asks.

"Now we get the gang back together."

The self-driving system sits in its metal case on the coffee table in Cassian's living room, quiet, inert. It looks like what it is—an old, obsolete computer system—and not something that's caused a man's death. Or all the rest of this trouble.

The guys are all staring at it with clouded expressions. Except for Cassian. He looks lighter, like an anchor's been cut from around his neck. He's not happy exactly, but more like he can see happiness ahead. Which is weird since he just confessed that one of his mentors probably killed his other mentor. But it also makes me lighter to see him taking charge, casting off his dark doubts.

"It has to be Oscar," he says, spreading his hands. "He's the only person who fits all the facts. He had access to the original system, access to my car in the time period before my crash, he's not a good enough coder to alter his kill switch, and… and there's a possible motive."

Gage sits back, his eyes narrowed. He's not combative, but he'll need more than this to believe. "Fine. I'll give you that he had access. Along with all of us and Morgan and Raven."

"Except that Morgan's code wouldn't be so sloppy," Gideon says.

"And Raven can't code at all," Bishop adds.

Gage works his jaw. "Still, motive? To kill his business partner and very best friend? It's not like Oscar profited when Ira died. We all did, so that leaves all of us as prime suspects."

"We are," Cassian says. "But look at what Oscar's done since Ira died."

Archer frowns. "He hasn't really done anything."

"Exactly." Cassian's jaw tightens. "They were having regular breakthroughs on the neuronal interfaces. Everyone thought they'd have something major very, very soon. Then Ira died and… nothing. Everything coming out of their company just stops. Oh, they keep making the chips they already developed, but there's nothing new or exciting or groundbreaking."

Gage sits up. "So it was all Ira's ideas and innovations all along? Then why kill him?"

"I don't know. That's what we'll have to find out next."

At Cassian's solemn words, Archer stirs. "The notebooks," he says. "You think Ira left some clues there."

"Or he left everything there," Bishop says. "He revised his will about six months before he died, and that's when he put the notebook bequest in. So he probably finished the notebooks around then. What was he working on at the time?"

Gage shrugs. "Something with Tynan."

"But not with Oscar?" Archer asks.

"I don't know," Gage says.

Cassian steeples his fingers. "Maybe he was planning on cutting Oscar out of whatever he was working on. He saw the potential for something really, really big and didn't want Oscar involved. Oscar figured it out and—" Cassian spreads his hands.

Bishop blows out a long breath. "And Tynan didn't say what it was?"

"Tynan didn't say shit about shit," Cassian says, his jaw

tight with anger. "We can't count on him. I don't know what's happened, but he's got his own agenda now and I can't figure it out."

Gideon makes a small snarling sound. "Fine. It's just us then. We go through the old servers, the notebooks, whatever we can remember, and piece together whatever this last project of Ira's was. If you're right and it is all in the notebooks, then he wanted us to have it anyway."

"We should also be looking for Tynan," Gage says. "Maybe he doesn't want to be found, but too fucking bad. We're going to need his notebook eventually anyway."

"The burglar," Cassian says. "Find her and you've got a lead on him. I'm sure of it. I'd bet Tynan's too paranoid now to entrust it to anyone he doesn't have a personal connection with."

Gage snorts. "Sure. Like I haven't already been doing that."

"And Oscar?" Archer asks quietly.

There's a long, hard beat of silence.

"There's nothing definite here," Cassian says eventually. "Nothing that would convince anyone."

Gage looks at him sharply. "So you're not sure?"

"No, I am. But… but we need more if we're going to take this to anyone outside this room."

I suddenly realize that I'm in the room. And Tess too. Somehow we've been drawn into this circle. It's an oddly satisfying feeling, for all that we're being drawn into solving a years-old murder by car.

"We keep it from everyone," Gideon says. "We keep an eye on Oscar"—he meets Gage's eyes—"make sure the girls stay safe, and when we've got the evidence, we bring it to Raven and Morgan. They're going to take it much, much worse than we did. And from there… we decide how to deal with Oscar."

A shiver runs over me at his tone. I'm guessing some of those solutions for Oscar are outside the bounds of the law.

They all nod solemnly.

After a moment, Archer gets up. "I suppose I should get back to work. Unless you guys know anyone who can translate gibberish?"

"Ask that translator you're on the panel with next week," Cassian suggests with a wicked smile. "She might speak gibberish."

Archer's mouth flattens. "I don't know why I let you talk me into that. I hate that kind of shit."

"Archer is going to be on a panel with a translator next week," Cassian says to my inquiring look. "They're going to debate the efficacy of translating via AI. It's great branding for him."

It is, but given how surly Archer is, Cassian also saw an opportunity to poke at his friend.

"That should be interesting," I say politely.

Cassian cracks out a laugh. "Oh yes."

"She's also an Instagram poet," Tess offers. "Axel Beck sometimes shares her poems."

Archer's expression goes hard as stone. "An Instagram… *poet?* How is that even a thing?"

"That should be the first thing you ask," Cassian says.

Gideon shakes his head as he reaches for Tess's hand. "Don't ask that."

Tess goes to him with a wide smile.

"I'm not that stupid," Archer mutters.

"Good luck," I say as he leaves.

Once they're gone, I give Cassian a severe look. "Did you set that up just to annoy Archer?"

He widens his eyes in mock innocence. "I would never. And seriously, it's great marketing. She's going to argue for human translations and he's going to argue for computer translations. People will eat it up."

"You would." I roll my eyes as he pulls me close and starts kissing my neck. "I'm beginning to think you like it when I scold you."

"Nope," he murmurs against the pulse hammering in my neck. "I *love* it. Keep going in that exact same tone—I'm almost there."

Laughing, I futilely smack at his shoulder as he lowers us to the sofa.

"Lawford is going to burst in on us," I say, my voice gentled. I can't keep up the other, not with the delicious things he's doing to me.

"He won't." Cassian undoes my pants, his fingers finding the soft skin of my belly. "He wouldn't dare." He lowers his mouth to taste where he touched. "But to be safe, be a good girl and don't scream."

I already know that's an impossible request, not with the bad boy I've chosen to love.

ABOUT THE AUTHOR

Raleigh fell in love with billionaire romance as a teenager thanks to Harlequin Presents. She fell in love with San Francisco in her twenties thanks to how charming the city was. And she fell for a coding genius thanks to how charming *he* was.

Naturally, she had to put all of the things she loved into her romances.

You can find her online at www.raleighdavis.com.

www.ingramcontent.com/pod-product-compliance
Lightning Source LLC
Chambersburg PA
CBHW030741110726
47900CB00008B/2405